Their Fathers' Lies

James Thurbin

Bright Pen

Visit us online at www.authorsonline.co.uk

A Bright Pen Book

Copyright © 2009 James Thurbin

Cover image by © Tony Salter

Cover design by © Jamie Day

All rights reserved. No part of this publication may be reproduced, stored in a retrieval system, or transmitted in any form or by any means, electronic, mechanical, photocopy, recording or otherwise, without prior written permission of the copyright owner. Nor can it be circulated in any form of binding or cover other than that in which it is published and without similar condition including this condition being imposed on a subsequent purchaser.

ISBN 978 07552 1197 5

Authors OnLine Ltd
19 The Cinques
Gamlingay, Sandy
Bedfordshire SG19 3NU
England

This book is also available in e-book format, details of which are available at www.authorsonline.co.uk

For Gaynor

Acknowledgements

To all British Soldiers past and present who have sacrificed so much for my freedom and made us all so very proud of our special country. Other Gentlemen of England do hold their manhoods cheap!!

All the terrific authors on this subject especially Lyn Macdonald, John Keegan, Peter Charlton, Richard Holmes, Terry Norman, Andy Simpson, Alan Clark, Vera Brittain, RC Sherriff and Siegfried Sassoon.

I would like to thank all those people who have, over the years, asked me 'How's the book going Jim?' It really was those folk who drove me on to finish.

I need to thank Tom, Roger and Ellie Stiles for their advice on the technical details which, before their involvement, were flawed!

My thanks to Tamara Osmond, Christine Thurbin, Beverley Thurbin, Julian Thurbin, Darren Higgins, Wendy Salter, Michael Trompetto, Hillary Barnet, John and Jackie Hamblin, Kay Degatis, Kim and Joe Anderson for the encouragement. Your words really meant so much.

Nick Templar…you know!

Tony Salter, for his design magic.

To my beautiful wife Gaynor without whom I would be nothing. All her encouragement, love and support gave me such an advantage.

Johnny, Michael and Juliet who are everything.

And my dear Father, who I know has never left me.

Their Fathers Lied

'If any question why we died
Tell them, because our fathers lied'
Rudyard Kipling

Prologue

Older men sometimes carry a dignity which younger men could never possess. Richard Turner had this quality in abundance. He had transferred his style into success in his business and family life and was a venerable friend to all who knew him.
In his younger days he was a soldier and fought in the First war. Only his wife knew of his real experiences, but his grandchildren pressed him for details, which, in his older years he was beginning to release, in small and censored measures.

He was sitting in the pleasant surroundings of a Gentlemen's club in Pall Mall. He knew the place well and was a prominent and active member. He had stayed here for the first time while on leave in 1917, as many young officers had at that time.
He looked out of the large windows onto Pall Mall where taxis raced to find their positions to turn left down Marlborough road towards the Mall and his mind drifted to his younger days, squinting his eyes as a heavy memory passed through like a pedestrian on the outside street.
'Afternoon Dickie.' He was startled by the arrival of his friend.

He was having lunch this day with a yet older gentleman. George Price was another old soldier from Turner's Regiment who had seen service in both wars but usually from a safer distance. He turned and greeted his old friend.

They talked about their families, the cricket and all the usual topics discussed during these lunches which occurred every three months or so.

After a brief lull in conversation, the slightly scruffier George Price blurted out a question, in a manner that suggested it was a question he had been waiting all afternoon to ask.

'Do you remember Billy Mercer?'

Major Turner was shocked.

'How extraordinary, I was thinking of him just before you arrived.' He paused. 'Billy Mercer, now that's a name I have not heard for a long time.' His eyes and thoughts were temporarily elsewhere.

'Yes, I remember Billy Mercer. There was a time when I thought of that man every single day'

He returned his gaze to his friend with a smile that held tenderness and a little regret.

Chapter 1

The thick smoke blended with the noise to give an atmosphere of a bustling London street on a foggy day. Clinking glasses, laughing, shouting, deep serious conversation. Scores of people forgetting troubles, drinking, drinking, brown ales, scotch, gin.

'Good Luck my boy'. He was just nineteen although these were far from unfamiliar surroundings.

He turned, smiled and finished his beer until he could see through the bottom of his glass. He paused for a while to take in the scene through this medium of thickened glass. The pub seemed no more blurred as his alcohol induced failing vision appeared to make the room spin at an accelerating rate. He closed his eyes but made things far worse.

'Yeah', he had already forgotten who had wished him luck. It was luck he needed for where he was going. Where he and his friends were going. The last leave before embarkation to Etables and then on to the front. The same destination as Alfie Roberts's son who was no more. He turned to Alfie who was usually in here on Fridays. Alfie was crying, sitting in this London pub, surrounded by men, but on his own, and crying. His son was a professional soldier who had been in the show since the start, but his luck ran out at Loos.

Billy Mercer barely knew his son, but he had known Alfie, before his life was ruined.

He began to stare.

Little Bobby came over to him and planted a drunken arm around him.

'We're gonna be alright aren't we Billy. Probably be all over before we get there'

'Hope not Bob', he turned giving Bobby a disdainful look 'What you on about?'

Bobby shrugged and looked at his friend and then looked at the others who were all present, all drunk and all sailing for France the next evening. There were seven of them going, seven passed medicals and basic training. Seven going to war.

Billy Mercer moved away, allowing Bobby's arm to slump down. He stumbled over to a table for some support for his decidedly unsteady frame.

'Sit down before you fall over son. Can't hold your drink. When I was your age I could……….' The cockney voice faded as he found a corner of a seat. He looked up to see another drink coming his way. The provider was wobbling and Billy saw the beer spilling in waves over the lip of the glass. Closer and closer it came, through the smoke and haze. It was almost dropped onto the beer soaked table. BANG!

Chapter 2

BANG! Another eighteen pounder shell exploded sending shrapnel spraying onto the wire. Smoke covered the field. Men's voices could be heard but shrieks of agony replaced the laughter. There were a dozen British soldiers pinned onto the wire almost like laundry on a washing line. Billy's eyes opened to reveal his terrifying plight, bleary, in a daze, half conscious. They closed again as he winced in pain. Agony like he had never felt. His whole body exploding, his head spinning, his ears bursting. Blood dripped into his eyes as he moved. He was stuck, caught in the wire like fish in a net. His eyes opened again to reveal the grey figures approaching. The shelling and gunfire had stopped, he hoped this was his rescue. He looked again to find he was wrong. These were German soldiers, bayonets glistening as they approached. He twitched to find his neck surrounded by a wire collar. His legs were both tied with wire which bit into his skin at every movement. The smoke was still thick but he could see the task the Germans were here to perform. The Sergeant of the Prussian Infantry pulled back his rifle and thrust the bayonet into the stomach of a trapped Englishman. A silent jolt was all that greeted the dreadful thrust, as the blade was withdrawn to spill the man's innards onto the muddy ground. The next man was found fully conscious. He cried, begged, sobbed, none of which impacted on the stone grey faces of the Prussians. This time they aimed for the neck, missing striking his mouth, tearing his lips, shattering his face. The next thrust found his neck as the soldier struggled like a harpooned whale. The cry could have been heard in England, where in a week's time it would surely be matched. They moved on to the next piece of laundry.

    Others in the line realised and struggled. Billy followed, the wire tightening around his neck. His hot steaming blood again covered his face but he knew he must escape. Every last piece of energy must be used to pull away. The pain was too much; could he not just wait for his fate, much easier, less painful? Yes that's the answer, his injuries were too bad, no energy to run even had he escaped his bindings. His eyes again closed, he was no longer cold, he almost smiled as he again drifted to sleep. This is it, only nineteen but glad to be out of this. Glad to be away from constant fear, cold, wet, hunger, rats, depravation, and brutality. Not what he expected. No glory here, nothing here, just death, pain and death. He must have lost too much blood , his neck wounds were leaking blood like a damaged hose. Just accept it, O hurry up. O Mum make it hurry up. He saw her face, like Alfie Roberts.

No, he would not let it; he cannot accept dying like an animal in an abattoir. He always had more fight than this. The only credit he had ever been given was for his fight. The boys down Bermondsey admired him for his fight. His mother was proud of his fight. Bollocks, I'll get out of this or die trying, German Fuckers. I'll fight these bastards. His eyes opened again. He pulled at his neck. The pain was unimaginable as he felt the barb rip his skin further. More blood. He knew the only way was one big rip, take the pain and pull back your head to release yourself. He saw his rifle on the ground beside him. Pull, Rip, do it, just do it. 1,2,3……..pull. Aaaaghh. No he was not free as he now felt he punctured more vessels in his skinned neck. Still trapped as the spring in the wire pulled him back. He imagined himself as a boy, being caught in brambles knowing that trying to release himself by unpicking the thorns with his fingers took too long. You have to just pull and accept the scratches. The Prussians were closer just 3 or 4 to go before him. The smoke drifted past to temporarily hide their image, but they were still there. The pain was so intense it could not possibly get worse. One more try. He pulled, away came a whole section of flesh as it ripped up to his ear like torn material. One more and he will be free. He pulled again and released himself. He tore away the wire from his hands and tunic, tearing both. The Prussians seemed not to have noticed as they continued bayonet practice. They now would have totalled six or seven. He tripped as the last piece grabbed onto his puttees and boots, but kicked himself free. Mud covered his wounds, he could hardly breathe without crying out with the pain. As he picked up his rifle, not knowing whether it was loaded or damaged, he had no recollections of even the previous week at that moment. As the smoke cleared a Prussian saw him and ran at him with his bayonet. Had they no rounds in their weapons? He grappled with the butt, pointed the rifle roughly in the direction of his attacker and let off a round, just two feet from the Prussian's head. The round entered just above the eye and took the remaining parts of his head clean off. The Prussian's eyes looked skywards where his soul quickly followed. Billy looked around him to find the remainder of a wood about fifty yards behind him. Was that what he was attacking or from where he attacked? He ran for this protection as the remaining Prussians gave chase. He cursorily let off new rounds from his hip, not knowing whether they hit. Rounds cracked past his ears and splashed the mud beside him, flattering their size with explosion like impacts as they hit the muddy water. The stumps were but thirty yards away as he stumbled, expecting nothing but death. More rounds pierced the air as the Prussians all fell like dominoes.

'Quick bud, quick over here, down for fucks sake, over heeeere'.

Welsh accents from nowhere. As the smoke cleared again taking spirits with it, he saw a waving arm from the crest of the splintered forest. The rifles spoke again this time accompanied by the rattling and ringing of a Vickers machine gun. The air was buzzing as though a beehive had been disturbed creating a picture like Dante's Hell. Billy continued to stumble towards the waving arm, finally making the distance after what seemed like a lifetime of evading sudden death. He fell into the shallow trench into the arms of a Welsh Infantryman.

He awoke again to find himself some distance from where he fell surrounded by wounded and dying men. The rifle fire had stopped, although the air was still punctuated by the occasional burst of an 8 inch shell. The forest seemed much thicker, offering protection to these wounded and helpless men as the light faded into twilight, bringing with it a shower of rain which refreshingly fell down on Bobby's ripped and damaged face. The pain in his neck had subsided somewhat although his entire uniform was brown with thick congealed blood. As his eyes focussed he saw the pale form of an older corporal staring into nothing. His life was finished on account of the fact that both his legs were missing. He was calmly breathing taking air deep into his lungs, exhaling slowly, hopefully to dull the pain. It seemed amazing to Billy that the feeling of resignation and despair was coupled with such calm. He could not help but stare. The wounded around the two were crying and crawling while these two were almost in a trance. He could smell the burnt blood and flesh hanging from his comrade's thighs. The rain was falling heavier now and seemed to roar as each drop splashed upon the covering foliage, tumbling down to hit tin. Surrounded by horror, pain, fear, despair.

With his eyes firmly fixed on the twisted figure of the limbless soldier, he heard a number of artillery rounds fly through the air. An unusual sound this one as he had already learned to differentiate between the various shells that fly these skies, by their sound alone. He did not recognise this sound. The several shells landed with a plop and failed to explode. Similarly useless shells to so many of those that fell from British guns on that fearful morning of July 1st on the Somme. There was just quiet now, many of the wounded had perhaps died, although the man opposite from him was breathing as before with his mouth wide open. He again became transfixed with the horror lying in front of him.

The silence was suddenly shattered by a mind wringing bell clanging and men shouting. He could not make out the cries but his blood froze as he distinguished the word gas. Panic ensued, sheer panic. Men screamed, cursed and wailed as they all fought to fix their clumsy masks just in time. He did not know whether he even still had his with him. He checked his belt webbing on his left and with horror realised it was not there. Resign yourself again boy, this is just too much. Sit and let it happen. He checked his right side and with utter relief found a folded piece of cloth which was his gas mask. By now he could hear the choking of those in front who had no time to fit the masks. He was unaware that humans could make such a sound and turned to see shadows darting around a smoky scene with a green mist creeping closer towards him. He fitted his protection as he turned to see most of the living around him had managed to do likewise. One had not, the corporal. He lay just as he had before the bells rang with the same expression. Bobby crawled over to him and ripped his mask from his waist. As he attempted to fix it to the corporal's face, he began to be restrained. 'Leave me son, for God's sake leave me…… please?' The corporal looked at him and smiled, resignation had won his internal battle. With the green mist just feet away, Billy stopped and realised. He should have fitted it anyway but something stopped him. He sat back and watched the corporal as he stared skyward, almost like Jesus upon his cross. Into your hands Father, I commit my soul.

Billy was suddenly immersed in the green mist which immediately bit into his lacerated neck. The pain demanded a scream but the mask would not allow it. He could now not breathe to satisfaction and wondered at the usefulness of these damned masks. He looked at the corporal and soon discovered how effective they were. Having taken one breath the man immediately flew into a blind panic. His withered stumps flipped around as he fumbled and struggled to find his mask. Accepting and facilitating his death by chlorine was no longer a desirable option as he squealed, making the same sub human noise as was all around. Billy again dived to his aid in a frantic attempt to help him fix the mask as his convulsions and struggles became all the more violent. He had taken several breaths by now, the chlorine mixing with the moisture in his lungs to produce a deadly concentrated acid which burned through the inside tissue of his chest. He splattered a mixture of mucus and blood out through his mouth, his eyes bulged as though they would shoot from their sockets at any moment. Still alive, still struggling this poor wretch still tried to prevent more of the vaporised acid from invading his body. Billy could hardly bear the scene he was witnessing, as he tried to do all he could to help the man. The best way would surely have been to put a bullet in his brain. With one final splutter, it seemed that what remained of his lungs flew from his mouth over the covered face of the younger man. The sound which accompanied was enough to drive a man insane as the corporal drowned in this sea of death. His struggles finally halted to leave the tortured face staring with eyes like golf balls at the sky. His mask fell to the ground and was full of the steaming mixture of acid, blood and mucus which bubbled and hissed as it lay by his side. It was hard to imagine a worse form of dying. His hands were smoking as the acid burned from this mixture. Billy himself began to choke as the mask inevitably leaked. All around him was death and writhing agonised bodies of fine men meeting cruel and horrific deaths. With the intense smell of chlorine in his nose, he picked himself up and stumbled to where the floating death had come from. Masked men were all around but there was the semblance of order here. A Lieutenant ordered him to sit, by various waving movements of his arms. Obeying his instructions he fell against a tree and tried to breathe slowly. It became easier and after a while he could hear voices, although he still could see very little through the dreadful deposit on his mask. With his neck giving him a fresh burst of agonising pain, he wiped the glass to see the faint sight of soldiers without masks, 'Thank God'.

He tore off his mask and gulped a breath as though finally reaching the surface from being submerged in water. Although the air was still full of the dull stench of chlorine, it still felt as crisp and fresh as sea air at dawn. When all the wounded were rounded up from the battered and bloody field, all those walking were instructed to walk the three miles to the casualty clearing station. This had been a disastrous day for the British Army, the 33rd Division in particular. The assault on High Wood was unsuccessful, with Regiments from all over the commonwealth suffering decimation. The appalling fate of Billy's regiment was still unknown to him as he wandered aimlessly towards his respite. Around him was nothing but death, men ripped apart by shells, heads taken off by Machine gun rounds, they always hit the head, and men whose lungs had burnt out and whose skin had already taken the yellow and thick form of a brightly coloured blanket. He felt as though he was in a dream, a terrifying dream, yet he paradoxically felt the need to sleep. O to sleep! His head was spinning as he stopped to throw the contents of his guts onto the muddied ground. His wounds again began to bleed, he could not take another step. Simon of Cyrene pulled him to his feet as he tried to continue his march. The men accompanying him had the look that can never be described or painted. Their souls had practically left their bodies. The smell was diabolical, the noise of rain deafening, the sights around him horrifying the pain he felt unbearable, the taste in his mouth unimaginable. All his senses terribly abused. He fell again, the sound ceased, pain stopped, smell died, taste disappeared and his vision blacked out.

Chapter 3

His name was Billy Mercer. He was born and bred in the South London borough of Southwark where he had spent most of his life dodging the law and running errands for the local business men cum politicians cum villains who would operate around the docks. They liked him for two reasons, he could think and he could fight. His parents were relatively respectable in this area, his Mother would teach dancing above a grocers shop by London Bridge, classes which were extremely popular and would attract many from the more affluent side of London. Clare Mercer was a successful dancer when younger and appeared in some West End shows where she met and married a fruit seller who she found she could not live without. His Father spent most of his life in the pub and Billy rarely saw him except for the times he ventured into his pub on Tooley Street. Billy had fought and won a bare knuckle contest in the Queen's Head and that was the one time where he saw pride in his Father's eyes. Granted that he gave his Father most of his winnings, but still there was pride at his win. Nice way for Billy to make a little extra cash. It was not too long after that his Father was killed by a Russian sailor from the docks in a row over a card game. His Mother was inconsolable for weeks, but Billy coped with it fine. No problem really.

Soldiering was something Billy would never have considered and he was certainly not the first in line responding to Kitchener's finger. It was just what every other young fella from the neighbourhood was doing and he would not have liked to have been thought a coward. Many of his generation had already joined when he dragged his closest friends with him to sign for the Royal Fusiliers. He was proud to wear his uniform around London and found he became more attractive to women. When he stole an officer's uniform and wore this in town, he was amazed how easily women and their underwear were parted, but that was Billy Mercer. Jimmy Moon, George Turpin, Reggie James, Pete Jackson, Charlie Pendry and even Bobby Taylor all passed their medicals. Bobby apart, the recruiting Sergeant seemed proud to show off this bunch as they all had exactly the qualities Britain needed, especially given some of the shower he had been forced to pass.

Chapter 4

The first few days of training resulted in a string of fights with other recruits, Georgie almost killing a recruit for which he was taken away only to return two days later with body bruises from his neck to his ankles. Nothing new to George, he lived for this kind of stuff. The injured recruit with the big mouth was never seen again. However, before long the platoon realised who was in charge and outside training it was not the Sergeant. Billy explained that they all expected to be ordered around and as long as nobody took the piss with fatigues, they should not take offence when given orders. These men, who had never allowed anyone to take liberties accepted this view as it was necessary if they were to go on this temporary adventure. Billy then asked the sergeant if they could meet in private for a gentlemanly discussion. The price Billy paid for this courtesy was unconsciousness for ten minutes as the only blow of the exchange also split his lip and blacked his eye. He was in the Army now, for fucks sake get used to it. The Sergeant became easier and although it pained him to admit it, Billy actually became rather fond of the northern twat. They all felt like the kids they were while crawling in mud and shooting rabbits on the range instead of the targets. A Court Marshall offence. The sergeant got two. Leave in Aldershot was ludicrous resulting in more violence and extra duties. None of the lads had done so much fighting but with the extra feeling of fitness and various regiments around it was irresistible.

Finally they were off to Etaples for combat training. The famous Bull Ring. To France at last. They were all amazed at the extent of the British Army. There was everything here, Artillery, Cavalry, Logistics, Catering, Engineers, Veterinary, Medical, everything. There were even sailors here, looking dreadfully incongruous in their uniforms. The training here was even harder with less than four hours sleep per night.

They were told that this is more than they should expect in the trenches. For the first time they heard the terrible sound of the guns, rumbling, softened like distant thunder. In the evenings they would stand transfixed facing east watching the flashes. He could not imagine how they managed to make so many shells as the flow was relentless. He started to think about exactly what he had let himself in for, he began to feel fear for the first time. He'd seen it in the faces of the others, especially Bobby. Poor Bobby, the runt of the litter but bitterly defended by them all. As he gazed east he saw again the face of the Scotsman. He had been resting on a grass bank, screaming some argument with Charlie about fucking a girl up the arse and whether it made you queer or not. The entire platoon was laughing as a company of Scots guards marched past. There was an immediate silence but Billy continued with his back to the road. 'You'd tear her apart' he naively cried but stopped and turned to discover the reason for the silence. He looked straight into the eyes of a young kilted soldier marching back from the front. There seemed so few for a company, fifteen at most instead of ninety. As he caught his eye he became trapped like a trout on a line. He couldn't pull his eyes away. He'd never seen such an expression, distant, horrific, the face of one who considers himself in a dream and not really living through this. He felt ashamed to be smiling, the smile slowly left his face. The soldier stared, telling him, warning him. Rough seas ahead. The others must be seeing the same look, why was he staring at him. He felt sick, still they stared. As the soldier's head began to turn, he broke the gaze and again stared forward. This was a living ghost, this man had witnessed Hell, his soul seemed to have left him leaving just a walking body. 'You'll no be laughing long, laddie' he almost heard the ghost whisper. What had he seen, what could possibly have such an effect on a man? The depleted ghost soldiers marched on, on to leave, to try to pretend that they did not have friends. Nobody spoke for what seemed like an age until they were summoned back for more bayonet training. Things were beginning to get serious now, they stopped talking about their intended heroics.

Bobby was starting to cause concern, he did not seem to be eating and was not making everybody laugh as he did. He looked so tired and was closing his eyes during bayonet practise. He was talking about London more and more, he missed his home. Army life was not for him. He'd be out of it soon.

Chapter 5

They joined the regiment in early June. The march to the front was something none of them would ever forget. They went from roads to paths to tracks to bogs. The shelling was becoming closer and closer, they were walking right into it. They eventually marched past the British guns with shirtless gunners working like slaves. The noise was deafening. Nobody expected the activity to be anything like this. Even the Sergeant looked shocked as they passed the ruined remains of houses and regiments. Even further they marched, shells falling not five hundred yards before them. Not a house remained standing, brick rubble and dust everywhere. Men running around, horses loose, equipment falling from broken bullet ridden carts. The whistling sound of approaching shells hit them for the first time. It amazed them how the flying shells were clearly visible as they flew overhead. So many different sounds they made as they flew. It was mentioned during training how to distinguish the high explosive and shrapnel shells by this sound. It seemed to make no difference, either will kill you if they land within 50 yards, the former by sucking out your lungs, the latter by tearing limbs clean off. How can men possibly live amongst this, but the nearby soldiers were calmly chatting, even laughing to one another around this pandemonium. They entered their first trench, still having over a mile before reaching the intended destination. On entering the trench they entered another world. Men were cooking food, drinking tea and rum. In the trench walls were further tunnels leading to dug outs where men lived and worked. Ammunition lay around like scrap wood, others stared as the Fusiliers walked through the crowded trenches. The sophistication of the trench network always surprised new troops, they were self sufficient villages with street signs, storage dumps, latrines, cook houses, hospitals, sleeping quarters and officer's messes. Nothing in the trenches was quite as grand as the Officers' mess. Utter madness. The noise was beyond deafening, being so close to exploding shells was utterly nerve shattering. Nobody at home would believe this, he thought to himself. He had his own perceptions as a civilian and he knew they were a long way from reality. As he meandered his way through the network he looked behind to check his friends. Reggie James with his jet black hair showing beneath his helmet and his unshaven face showing his defiance to military rules. He was in his element, totally excited, longing to boast of the experience. Jimmy, constantly ducking looked terrified, his piercing blue eyes darting. Georgie, unfazed walking straight, eyes front. Charlie attempting to cover his terror and attempting to hold his muscles from soiling his self. Pete, whose head was inches closer to the parapet than the rest shrieking fuck that, fuck this at every impact before a corporal demanded he stop, but being told to fuck off as well. Then Bobby. He was almost crawling forward, in a state of disbelief, making a constant groaning like a sulking child. They were urged to stop by the young Second Lieutenant at an area where the parapet lowered. As they stood, Billy again turned to look behind him. Things turned quiet as he heard a smack and turned to see a flow of sand falling down from a supporting sandbag to the muddy floor. He paused and stared with a puzzled gaze just as he heard a smacking sound and another flow of sand started just by. 'Sniper, Sniper!'

They all dived down to the floor except Pete. He remained standing and slowly raised his hands to his face which was no more. At the back of his head was a dark red hole. He eventually fell backwards with the sand of the sandbag continuing its flow onto his bloodied and dead face. Thick dark blood flowed from his face and his head, a red pool forming rapidly beside him. His helmet was untouched but just helped direct the blood flow to join with that from his face. Silence seemed to pervade as they all stared open mouthed at their mutilated dead friend. Bobby cried out for all his lungs were worth, no longer being able to contain his anguish.

These men were travelling up the line to take part in the struggle for High Wood during the fearful Battle of the Somme. They would soon be going over the top. But one would live.

Chapter 6

White, all he could see was white. He heard voices, talking in civilised tones, no shouts, no crashes but peaceful calm. He felt good as though waking from a long restful sleep. Turning his head he found thick bandages up to his mouth, restricting able movement. He realised he was in hospital. Not dead, in hospital. White sheets, white walls, white nurses. This was no casualty clearing station but the clean, sterile environment of a hospital. Here he was to recover. The Sergeant would be informed that Billy was fit to talk and be summoned to debrief the young soldier on the events of the previous week. Although Billy had witnessed the affair, his recollections were non-existent at this time.

'I was ordered not to take part in the attack. Not too happy about it but at least I am here to tell you'

Billy saw the look in Sergeant Pike's eyes. Although just over thirty he had the appearance of an old man with drooping saddened eyes showing pity and a hint of disbelief.

'All dead mate, all dead, we didn't manage to get any back, the wounded were all slaughtered where they lay. All fucking dead'

'But…. What....'

'They hadn't cut the fucking wire again, you all ran straight into it, I saw it all through the periscope. After that it was just fucking target practise.'

'Everyone? No, someone would have got through, surely. Bobby what ….Jim? All of them, no were they all with me on the wire?'

'Most didn't get that far, the Hun knew of the attack, set up the machine guns and ..well. I can't think how you managed to…

Billy sunk back into his pillow, gazing at the ceiling. This could not possibly be, there must be a mistake, surely his friends were still on this earth. No, no it cannot be. London, he thought of London, what would it be without them? London was all about them. Bobby's mother, how on earth would she cope with this? Nobody ever thought some would actually die. Images came back, Germans bayoneting men on wire. Bodies blown to pieces actually being hit by shells. The whole earth erupting like in a heavy rainstorm but with fire and mud not spray. All of them dead, he felt too shaken to cry.

'…. Back to the division for NCO training.'

'Mercer, are you listening to me, NCO training. The division needs NCOs, I've put your name forward, the wounds will heal in a matter of months at which time you're to join the 9th Battalion.'

'Yeah, yeah'. He saw that the nurses were all circumspectly looking at this encounter, they'd had the brunt of this attack, it was already a great talking point how a battalion had been practically wiped out. Even in this war that was quite unusual. For most it was their first sight of action. Pitiful, just pitiful.

Ironically the chlorine prevented his neck becoming gangrenous but he had still lost so much blood that his life was in danger when he reached the casualty clearing station. He'd also had a piece of shrapnel in his back which had narrowly missed his spleen. They had considered sending him back to Camberwell but the voyage would have probably killed him. Instead he lay in a hospital in Calais with English and French nurses who he would ordinarily have attempted to seduce. Not now though, not now. He could hardly bring himself to talk to other patients, his world had been shattered, torn apart. Nobody thought anyone would die, not die. Oh Jesus, Oh Jesus. He had a visit from his mother but hardly said a word, just stared at the wall thinking of Bobby's mother. Clare lied and told him she had not heard from her. She was content to see that her boy's wounds were healing and he had not turned insane. But oh how she wished she could take her baby home, take her only baby home and protect him from these officers, this army and this country's pride. She wept on the boat home which also carried wounded, by God was it her who would lose her mind?

Three years ago she lost her husband to violence, she could not bear losing her boy and become like so many others whose only contact with their children was through psychic mediums? Oh Jesus make it stop.

Chapter 7

Just twelve weeks after his baptism of fire, Billy Mercer was declared fit again for military action. He had a scar which ran from his ear to his mid shoulder and a painful scar on his back. With his uniform on his wounds were inconspicuous, his light brown hair and deep piercing blue eyes, which were almost violet, still making him a fine specimen. The training had further increased his upper body muscular mass and at six feet tall he still cut a dashing figure although he could not shake the slight limp. England's best his mother always told him. No, England's best lay in pieces on French soil which the rain, wind and shells would soon clear away.

Off he went to begin NCO training to gain his two stripes. For the first time he became an attentive student, it seemed that his character was hidden deep in his dull and sombre eyes. Suddenly during section Infantry tactical training he would feel a lump in his throat, and torture himself by forcing memories of his days in the sun upon his tired and wounded mind. He even wanted to sob as he saw their faces, smiling, always smiling. Fine, dear men. All dead.

The awarding of his stripes was a formality, before he knew it he was joining the 9th Battalion. It was December 1916. When he met the regiment it was cold, very cold. He had but one day's worth of real action, yet he felt a veteran, especially when he turned twenty. He felt he could live with these people. The young subaltern seemed inexperienced and terrified, like all subalterns he had seen, but the men, mostly from North East London seemed no different from his old pals. North London was always considered a shit hole and he enjoyed travelling north when younger to thrash a disrespectful bunch. However, he took to the men in his section straight away, they were a hilarious group. The first time he met them he had walked along a track to where his company were bivouacked in an orchard near a farmhouse. As he approached he was greeted with the sound of hysterical laughing and arrived to see three men throwing apples up to the window of the house. To his surprise and distinct amusement, he looked up at the window to see the arse of a young woman gaping out, being bombarded by apples. They were apparently chatting to her previously and began to throw her apples to eat, added a bit of English persuasion and the young French girl thought she was awfully witty by agreeing to their request. As they hit their mark there was a loud smack which was greeted with cheers and laughs from the whole company. Indeed an artillery regiment that had been passing stopped to watch the spectacle and a couple even joined in. As Billy approached he saw a juicy big apple laying to his left, picked it up, launched it only to see it miss, hit the shutters and bring the whole wooden shutter frame down. With this the arse disappeared and a struggle ensued inside the room. Out poked the face of an old woman screaming in French at these disgraceful English youths. She turned to make her way down the stairs leaving a weeping young girl, now too embarrassed to show her face, least of all her backside to her awaiting frenzied fans. They turned to look at Billy who simply raised his eyebrows and shifted his gaze to the door of the house from which the hysterical old woman would soon appear. She did indeed appear at the same time as a Captain approached to find out what the commotion was about. As he turned the corner he was struck clean in the face from a blow from the woman's stick as she screamed and yelled at the unsuspecting officer. This act was met by a roar of amusement by the waiting troops. The captain turned with a plaintive look as further blows ran down onto his head. He was inwardly begging one of the men to rescue him but spasms of laughter prevented anyone from lifting a finger to his aid. The assault continued as the men started to disappear in order not to face the Court Marshall that would surely have followed. As the men settled he noticed the three originally throwing the apples sat together, the only ones who did not seem to be still laughing over the episode. It appeared that this kind of caper was not out of the ordinary at all. One of the men sported an old colonial style moustache and to his amazement appeared to be smoking a pipe. This character, as he was to learn, was known by everyone as 'the Kings Road Pipe'. A resident of the Chelsea Street, he would have ordinarily joined the officer class but frankly was too wild. His Father, who had despaired of him years ago, did not lift a finger to help as he could have quite easily. What was apparent was that even with his extreme aristocratic accent, he fitted in perfectly with all the working class soldiers and was loved by all of them. He would call everyone, even officers 'young man' and was rarely bothered due to his connections which he would never use anyway. He had the driest yet quickest sense of humour of the whole regiment and as well as being popular for his character, would receive the most satisfying parcels from his dear mother who did worry so. In these parcels were just about every luxury a soldier could hope for, she would even regularly send pyjamas for his friends. He had a huge inheritance bound for him and was known to all the ruling classes. One of the most likeable most amusing men Billy had ever known was the Kings Road Pipe, interested only in fun and laughter. And his pipe. He was determined to join up and show his father, who had been an officer, that his life was at least a little worthwhile. Secretly the rejection from his father ripped him apart. Piers Montpelier was his amusing name yet he did not receive the slightest ridicule for the way he spoke, acted or smoked. Nobody abused the Kings Road Pipe or KRP as he was known. He puffed away on his pipe lying back staring at the sky, a wry grin as he seemed to be planning his next jest. He seemed happy with the world, but, he had not seen the front yet, things would have to change then. What a pity that such fine interesting men had to endure what lay ahead without even the slightest idea as to what it was really like.

'What was it really like … in the Great War?'

Among the other new group who caught Billy's eye and friendship was Paulo Mendini. Brought over from Italy as an infant he had worked in the flower market at Covent Garden. The enduring feature of his character was his optimism and enthusiasm for just about everything he ever did. His cheerfulness was the kind that would occasionally annoy people as a serious situation sometimes warrants appreciation of that fact, but one would never get that from Paulo. He even mentioned his joining up as a mere aside to his parents both of whom hit the roof at the news. Neither understood why he would wish to fight for a foreign country, but that was where he differed from them in that he felt slightly English whereas they were so Italian that they hardly spoke English. Paulo's reasons for joining were from boredom. There must be more to life than carting fruit around and stories he had heard all involved adventure. So with these thoughts in his head off he went to Stoke Newington with three pals none of whom passed the medical. When he arrived at the regiment he knew nobody but was soon befriended by the Kings Road Pipe, a man he was instantly keen on. He found military life to be perfectly bearable and enjoyed the weapons and fitness training. Another recruit he found common ground with was Johnny Mason, a small time crook from Tottenham. Mason was a career criminal and had stayed at his Majesty's pleasure a number of times. He knew that his next pull would involve an unjustified very long term so thought a spell with the army would take the heat away from him for a while. Besides, the regime could not be more onerous than prison life and there might be some nice pickings in France. Mason knew where to fence any product and had a large network of contacts who could sell anything. He had not yet had his large touch; he kept getting caught before the big jobs came his way. Just as well as he would be caught for them as well most probably and he wouldn't see daylight till he was over forty. But this fact was lost on him. If you can imagine a petty criminal in your mind, then you are thinking of Mason's appearance. Weasel like face, shifty eyes, thin and underfed looking, almost as if he had spent a bit of time in Fagin's den. But a man of the world who had been around a bit. And a good friend who paradoxically was loyal to those he counted as friends. Honour amongst thieves? Probably yes.

These were the leading roles for the platoon that Billy found himself in as a corporal. His role was one of heading a section but the platoon all worked as one and most NCO responsibility was reserved for the sergeants.

It seemed that the war had so far been no more than a joke to these soldiers. At every turn they had contrived to create an amusing situation and were quite ruthless in their selection of victims. Every piece of leave they were afforded was spent in riotous behaviour ending up in one of the many brothels which sprang up in Northern France. In stark contrast to Billy's late friends there was no interest here in fighting other regiments or the local French. Such antics would only serve to interrupt drinking and shagging and such interruptions were highly inconvenient. Around this company he started to live again, although the terrible pain of his loss would always weigh him down. Whilst in the middle of a joke he would be hit with guilt as his conscience told him he should really never laugh again. He often wondered what Reggie and George and the boys would have made of this mixed bunch of lunatics. Not much probably. They would have not taken well to Sergeant Pearce who was no more than a bully. Although he remained distant to Billy Mercer, there were many young privates for whom he made life hell, Private Caldwell, who was the retiring type, in particular. That was what was so cruel, that these men were hundreds of miles from home, cold, hungry, scared and constantly tired and yet they had to put up with such an NCO as this prat. Billy could anticipate an incident with this man.

Chapter 8

After a month spent behind the line, training, digging and marching, the 4th Platoon C Company 9th Battalion Royal Fusiliers, part of the 12th Division of the V1 corps, moved up the line to face the Germans at the ridge at Arras.

The march to the front was almost identical and as horrifying to the last one. He saw the faces of the men change as they neared the guns, as they felt the percussion and heat on their faces. The only real indifference was shown, of course, by the Kings Road Pipe. Staring straight ahead puffing away, he even fell out of line to reload, with total impunity. A twenty four year old acting like a sixty year old aristocrat. Onwards they marched, under the terrible howl of the guns, although there were incoming shells. It was Billy who worked out the trajectory of the eighteen pounder which was heading straight for them. He yelled to the men to take cover as they all broke rank and dived to the side of the road. Billy landed near the Subaltern whose shocked face gave away his total uselessness in this situation. As always there was relative silence immediately following the explosion and then the inevitable screams of those hit. In the middle of the road was a five foot crater, around it were pieces of uniform containing the remains of what were four or five men. There were yells of 'Fuckingggg Hell' as men tried to come to terms with what had happened. Billy was the first up, calling for a medic. As he got to the road he kicked a helmet on the floor only to realise that it still contained the head of its owner. Sergeant Pearce, of all people, looked up at them all as the tin helmet that contained his head rolled on its brim across the road. The Subaltern moaned as one who is about to jump off a cliff into the sea, and fell to his knees. He vomited all his stomach as the face in the helmet stared. Perfectly preserved with a diagonal cut from his chin on one side to his lower neck on the other. His eyes still open, with a....pleasant look upon his face. Pity the poor fucker who is to clear this mess up. As they waited Billy chatted to KRP who was picking out the gruesome sights which lay before them. From behind there was a laugh, had to be Paulo and of course it was, laughing about something or another. A Captain from the RMC was on the scene quickly as the gaps in the roll call identified the dead. Although shells were falling still, some semblance of order was restored as another Sergeant gave the order, or told the subaltern to give the order to march away. The regiment details and wounded were left with the Captain whose job it would be to co-ordinate the dead and wounded and report to the regimental headquarters. Still the survivors marched, the platoon already down by nine. After an hour they reached the trenches and were shown to their dug outs. Through sheer obstinence Billy ensured that he was barracked with Paulo, KRP and Johnny Mason.

As they settled in they noticed a civilian, standing in the trench with an odd looking contraption on a tripod. The man was turning the handle and shouting at men to look. This was a moving image camera and all the troops gathered and cheered in an attempt to get themselves filmed. The camera was pointing straight at Billy who returned its gaze almost like a rabbit in headlights. This film would one day be shown at theatre halls and all its viewers would think they had an idea of trench life. Men whose lives were close to ending would live forever in celluloid. The camera man strangely agitated him as he turned away back into his dug out.

Life in this trench consisted of six hours on two hours off over the twenty four hours of six days. The time awake was taken up with digging fresh dug outs, which Billy's group contrived to avoid, along with patrols and sentry look out duties. They were all so tired and felt they could not cope with the pace. Shelling was constant and no less terrifying than it had always been. Men continued to be picked off by snipers as they crouched round fires eating food which did nothing other than keep men alive. Sleep came everywhere, even while attending to the call of nature which was carried out on a charming rusty pole which ran the length of an unused trench line. The smell throughout the whole trench system was awful, men became used to living like caged animals and soon began to act like them. It rained constantly and the feeling of being wet and cold was the most usual state a soldier on the Western front was in. All just wanted a clean go at the Hun, all except those who had tried this enterprise.

Chapter 9

It was the Kings Road Pipe who gladly announced that the company were all to go for a week's R and R, twenty miles behind the lines. He had been talking to a Major 'with whom he had been to school' who gave him the news. No single prospect on earth could have been more gaily received, although this was common before a large scale frontal assault was planned. It was agreed that the only goal of Billy and his pals would be to get fucked and pissed as many times as was humanly possible in the week. A local village with a bar and a brothel was all that was required. They left the trenches under shell fire to be replaced by a company of Scottish troops who they passed when leaving the trench system. These were veteran troops who again showed the signs in their eyes alone. As they left they boarded, to their amazement, a double decker bus which chugged its way happily along the straight Roman roads westwards, passing bombed out villages and stray cattle. The roads were full of military traffic through which it took half the day to get past.

Eventually, at first light, they reached an evacuated bombed out chateau which was to be their lodging for the next week. They were not far from the town of Aubigny where they would venture every night in search of French women. They found that two other companies were occupying their lodging, as soon as they arrived they took no notice, found a warm corner and slept wonderful, deep, longed for sleeps.

It was an indictment on trench life exactly how much sleep a front line soldier would get when allowed. It was some fifteen hours later, deep into the following night that they woke and prepared themselves a breakfast that dreams are made of. KRP broke open all his supplies and the meal was finished off with champagne. These were the good times.

What a sight they were as they shaved and prepared themselves for a night's revelry.

Arguments abound, uniforms brushed, boots cleaned and that crank KRP's moustache waxed. With a veritable glow of anticipation they set off on the two mile walk for town.

Paulo was prematurely boasting of his conquests which would surely follow as he was such a good looking man. With his jet black hair, olive skin and Mediterranean romance, he would not struggle. The most incredible aspect of Paulo's character was his love of life. Nobody had ever heard him complain about any aspect of the soldier's plight. This was indeed unusual as moaning and complaining were developed into a fine art during the war. Everybody complained about the officers, the food, the weather, the boots, the weapons, the fatigues, the sleep, the lice but never Paulo. Something to be really proud of that, Billy always thought. Instead Paulo only laughed and played like a young puppy. When asked if he felt it was cold, he would only answer 'it's starting to get warmer'. There would later be an expression 'he's one you'd want with you in the trenches', well Paulo was it.

Half drunk already on brandy from KRP they arrived at the town, being immediately warmed by the sound of music and laughter which seemed to come from every part. It seemed that the whole British Army were enjoying this night. As they passed through the streets they came across just about every infantry regiment the British had, there were even Indian soldiers here and about. These soldiers were matched by what appeared to be the entire population of France's girls. This was one party town, exactly what the brass had contrived to create. Give the boys some good time before what is to follow. Nobody, of course, realised. A drunken Australian stumbled past and puked into the side of the road. Right boys lets get going.

They entered a crowded smoky bar and each man quickly got himself a bottle of the very poor house wine. What they saw inside this place appealed to all of them. Everywhere were working women already with the residue of countless men his cock still up the girl, pretending to whip her as a jockey does. The bar tender had seen enough and came running round the bar with a club which he began to use to strike blows onto the back of Paulo. The old romantic threw a punch at his assailant as the whole bar was exposed to the hilarious spectacle of a full blown fight, with the poor girl continuing, despite her efforts to escape, to be fucked. Some of the girl's fellow professionals then joined in the fray and before long the whole place was like a riot as fellow soldiers joined in on both sides of the argument. Paulo was fighting like an alley cat, having finally released the young Frenchwoman who by now was almost beside herself in shock and humiliation. The only male individual not involved in the fighting was the Kings Road Pipe who continued to conduct a deep conversation, in perfect French, with a young tart, who incidentally had his cock in her hand. The brawl drifted from one side of the bar to the next, like the tides of the sea, until eventually bodies started falling out of the door. Time to call it a night.

from all over the empire inside them. That didn't matter, they were all goddesses to them. The group made their way towards a piano which was being played, rather poorly, by a corporal. His drunken friends were singing along to some private song.

'Right, that's enough of that old shit. Move along boy, c'mon, move along for fucks sake.' Mercer was shouting over the din of the bar as the reluctant corporal was evicted from the chair. 'Pipe, give us a number'. He had no reason to believe the KRP could play the piano, but he'd have bet all the tea in China he could. And he would have won the unusual wager, for, of course, he could play and play like a virtuoso. Flicking back the seat of his jacket, as though he were wearing tails he took his position.

'I thank you. The song I will play is of love and true romance,' he announced over the din.

The bar seemed to quieten as the men turned to see the well spoken gentleman on the piano. They assumed he was an officer but upon inspection realised he was a mere private. A few disapproving comments were made, yet still he held his hand up, a lion tamer amongst these young lions. 'What's e fuckin' up to?' they called disdainfully but he had their attention. 'Love and true romance? What the..'

He smashed his hands on the keys, the room went quiet.

'I knew a wench with a minge like a trench……..' He sung and played and was greeted with the most hysterical laughter. He finished the whole disgusting song to the chants of Encore! Encore! At a stroke he had captured the audience, all the nicer girls, ones making a charge or not, were all over them within minutes. They played and drank themselves into a stupor, each going their separate ways into the chambers behind thick velvet curtains. Half way through the evening there was a woman's yell from behind the curtain which eventually collapsed to reveal Paulo fucking a whore, a rather nice looking whore, from behind but standing up. He was trying to manoeuvre here out into the bar to show the lads. Wheheeey, went the cheer from the Italian as the poor girl desperately tried to free herself. He pigeon footed along, with

Chapter 10

Billy woke with the enviable knowledge that he had a day ahead of him with nothing to do at all. No digging, no latrine duty, no mud, no whizzbangs crashing around his head, no sentry duties, no stand to, no artillery barrages. Nothing, just to lie around, play cards, wonder back into town and relax.

After a very pleasant breakfast with KRP, Paulo and Mason, they all decided to walk down to the river to find a nice place to fish and find a nice lunch.

As they approached the village they were met by an old boy who tried to sell them some cured ham that he had. In KRP's perfect French it was explained that they wanted to fish and have a nice lunch, for which he would be amply rewarded if he could so provide from this village. Within minutes he retuned with fishing gear for them all and they enjoyed an unusually warm early spring day, talking about home and what would become of them after the war. None of them caught a single fish and they started to doubt whether there were even fish in the river when the old boy of the village was back, beckoning them in for lunch. He took them through the town, where other soldiers were aimlessly walking around, in vain trying to find something of interest to do. Some found four discarded fishing rods by the river and all caught nice fish.

After a long walk through the town, the old boy announced that they were privileged to be dining at the local Mayor's house. A Mayor in name alone, Monsieur Bartan now made a tidy income serving high class meals to British Officers in his fine manor house which should have been taken over and used as some form of headquarters but somehow this old fool retained full use of his grand abode. What a place it was. This man was clearly retaining a handsome income while all the French around him were either dying in battle, or starving through lack of provisions and forced to survive like scavengers off the British Army stationed nearby.

Monsieur busy bollocks as he became known introduced the four to the supercilious Mayor who looked disapprovingly at their lack of officer status, but a few words from KRP earned them a table as they entered a large, finely decorated ballroom that was performing the office of a fine restaurant. Many officers were there, tucking into disappointing food, but as this was an unofficial restaurant, there was no restriction to officers alone. They were led to what was without doubt the worst table in the place as busy bollocks lingered around the Mayor until he received the paltry payment afforded to him for every group he brought.

An attractive waitress appeared with a torn paper which was the menu and the KRP ordered for them all, shrieking with delight when he viewed the wine list.

'I can't believe he has these wines here, a chateau Lafite 1900, Margaux 1900? There were only 29,000 bottles made of that, and this ponce has some of them.'

He called over the mayor and conducted a long conversation with him, doubting whether he had the wines he claimed. The mayor became animated at this aspersion and the KRP told him quite plainly that if he had a Haut Brion 1864, then he would buy one. He did and therefore KRP did, at 121 Francs. Outrageous price, almost 5 pounds. That was expensive for a London restaurant at peace time. With a sarcastic grin, the sardonic mayor brought out the bottle, insisted on payment before opening the bottle, did not even decant it and walked away laughing at these English fools. Billy was stunned, not only at the price, but at KRP's ability to take out of his pocket French notes that amounted to a fortune.

'Mother does worry so' he smiled as he leaned over to allow himself to return what was left of his currency to his pocket. The KRP seemed the least perturbed by the insolence of the mayor as he was keen to try the wine. It truly was superb and to the amazement of all, not least the officers dining close by, KRP ordered another when the first was consumed. The food hardly matched the wine although that too was also overpriced.

KRP would not hear of anyone contributing to the bill as the four walked out not thanking any Frenchman nearby.

While walking back slowly, Mason observed 'Fucking French, profiting on soldiers while we do the dying for him. Bastard!' He paused. 'He must have some cellar down there though.'

They all reacted in exactly the same way, with exactly the same in mind.

And so it was that the four of them conspired to relieve the pompous profiteering French Mayor of his entire wine collection. This was Mason's world and they all conceded to him on all aspects of the operation. While the Mayor slept and his large dogs fed on Bully beef, they gained access to his cellar and quickly realised exactly what kind of cellar this man had. They slowly but carefully liberated over 60 cases of some of the best wine ever created. Lafite, Latour, Graves, Romanee Conti, Cheval Blanc, Petrus, just about everything. The team had a fine sommelier on hand in the form of the KRP who gave the nod on which was worth taking and which was not. It took them almost all of the night, but just two days after, the KRP finally managed true value for the ten pounds he had spent on the Mayor's wine. His estimate for the value of this wine was in the region of £750, and this would be a good price even to a fence, whom Mason claimed he already knew who sold black market goods to restaurants in Mayfair. £750 was enough to buy 150 suits from the finest tailor in London that was the value of this stock.

It was starting to get light, even so early in the year, when they finished burying their treasure. Billy even wrote a treasure map, indicating the correct distance from the old birch tree in a copse situated just two hundred yards from the wine's former home, but the scarred land was covered with rotting leaves and nobody who was not involved with its burial would ever know its location.

They returned to their lodgings covered in early spring

mud and tried to sleep but sleep was difficult. At least one of them would burst into solitary laughter, starting the others off as the thought of what they had achieved and the prospects it brought warranted excitement which manifested in laughter. 'O do stop it Mason, for God's sake' in KRPs aristocratic tones then more laughter. How they laughed. Laughed and laughed and laughed. Mason finally had his large touch.

The, not so sardonic, mayor appeared in the camp the next day in a sense of, one could say, agitation. He demanded an audience with the highest ranking officer which was merely a captain who spoke no French and his complaint fell on deaf and ignorant ears as his face gradually turned more and more of a healthy hue until it appeared that the blood would soon burst out of his face. Mention was made of a Canadian garrison billeted at the other side of the village but the mayor was convinced he knew who would have taken his wine, but was not allowed access to the camp.

The captain, who himself had been stung by the extent of the prices at the Mayors place, eventually lost patience with the man, told him that many of his fellow Frenchmen had lost far more than a few bottles of wine and told him to piss off. This he did, hitting old Mr busy bollocks with his riding crop as he did, as though it was somehow his fault, which it probably was! He'd lost his fishing gear for him too.

Three copies of the treasure map were made. Each now had a copy and an agreement was made that if anyone was to not make it home, his share would go to the rest. None had family so this was considered the best solution. The true idea was for a trip back when this madness had stopped and they could all retrieve their bounty, drink a few bottles and then be rich men. For a while anyway. It is nice to have such a thing to fall back on! How nice it will be when the war ends. Not all the wine was buried. A few bottles were kept for those special occasions.

Chapter 11

The R and R that the 9th Battalion had was successful. The men had their minds distracted, their uniforms thoroughly cleaned, their bodies well nourished and refreshed and their courage revived. But, R and R cannot last for ever and the battalion was mustered for their march back to the front. Back to Hell, where they would be taking part in the next offensive operation around Arras.

It was during the march back to the front that Billy was truly confronted with the sensational industry that war was. Everywhere he looked there were thousands of men, more men than he had ever seen in one place at one time and although they were still several miles from the front lines it surprised him that this move was being undertaken without any regard for secrecy. The many aeroplanes flying overhead must have included German planes and any observer would have plainly seen the movement of hundreds of thousands of troops, equipment and more artillery than Billy had ever witnessed being dragged through the muddy tracks by weary and underfed horses. There were again many regiments from different parts of the world. On a rest, the Fusiliers found themselves lying on a grass verge for thirty minutes. While some slept, an Australian division marched past and also chose this spot for rest. The Australians seemed very large and fit, all of them seeming to possess an athleticism that was lost on the British soldiers. To match their large physical appearance was the volume of noise they made. Some unamusing event had them all laughing and screaming and pushing each other around, some falling by Billy and his group. Billy was eyeing them all with contempt. He wanted to act against this lot.

'Why can't that fucking lot quieten down?' Billy asked deliberately loud enough to be heard.

'O calm down Billy, just relax dear boy' KRP was laughing in his reply.

Very quickly the British had their response

'You actually say that, you Poms? Actually say "Dear Boy"? What a load of wankers you pathetic lot really are.'

That was enough. Billy was on his feet, glad for the opportunity to deal with him, very glad. The Australian in question stood firm, grinning as he watched Billy rise. He wore the Australian Slouch hat and was several inches taller than Billy with a healthiness about him that Billy had lost a long time ago. He was dark haired and tanned, suggesting a recent Middle East service

'No, Billy, leave him.' KRP attempted to prevent the unpreventable.

'Leave him? What? D'ya hear that boys?' He looked to his mates who by now were on their feet.

'You'd better sit down real soon mate or you'll never get up again,' the Australian continued.

The whining tang of his accent may have attracted the ladies, but just annoyed Billy further. There was no need for a verbal response.

'Roight you Fucker' the Australian began a sentence he did not intend to finish. He threw a laboured, haymaking punch which was easy to avoid and gave Billy the confidence that this man was no fighter. Billy leaned back to his right to dodge the blow, which gave him the perfect position and leverage to throw his own, well timed right hand. As the punch connected clean on his nose, he was then positioned to his left which allowed him to move his feet and generate full power on a left hook which hit the stumbling Australian, almost immediately after his first blow. In comical fashion the victim's head pounded back and his right leg flew in the air, resembling an intoxicated flamingo for a moment. Then he was down, unconscious before he hit the ground.

Billy was pleased with both shots, his fists were throbbing already, a good sign.

'Woow' went the cry from all the soldiers gathered nearby.

'It always was easy knocking out a fucking mug!' Billy stood triumphantly over his stricken prey, like David, missing only his sling!

A number of the Australians lurched forward to avenge their friend's humiliation when every English soldier in the vicinity rushed in to join the fray. Before any further contact was made, the sound of pistol fire sounded and they turned to see a group of Officers shooting in the air.

'Stop it you fools. We have German quarrels enough!'

Billy escaped into the melee of men and within moments his Battalion were ordered to march on. He could still hear Australian cursing as they marched away and the first hundred yards of the march was accompanied by hysterical laughing. They marched for hours, thinking only of their next chance to rest.

It was the KRP who pointed out a line of large metal hulks with many men standing around. These machines were the tanks they had heard of and while given a few moments rest from the march, they all ventured over to examine the beasts. A very supercilious young officer was not forthcoming with information but they were told that the next push would be bound to succeed with the help of the tanks. All the soldiers manning them were cavalry types, one of whom recognised the KRP. It was satisfying as this Captain ordered the unhelpful officer to allow Billy, Johnny, Paulo and KRP to look inside. The Captain seemed particularly fond of KRP and Billy wondered what that was about. There was so much to the KRP, so much Billy wanted to learn about as he constantly surprised everyone with his knowledge and contacts yet was always so modest and strangely interested in what must have been the banal stories that other soldiers told.

After this break they fell back in and continued their journey to the front. They marched for eighteen hours, only stopping twice to eat and rest and relieve themselves by the side of the track. The weather had turned cold for late March and there was the odd flake of snow in the air. They all longed to get to some trench and collapse into slumber but it appeared they 'had miles to go before they slept.' Everyone began to complain and shout out at the officers, many of whom were on horseback. Everyone, that is, apart from Paulo who retained his casual smile as he trudged along with thirty pounds of kit on his back like he was strolling through a park on a Sunday afternoon. The night turned darker, the weather colder and the ground muddier but eventually they found shelter in the reserve trench and finally found the luxury of four hours sleep. They were awoken by the sound of heavy artillery as a bombardment that was to last five days began.

More shells were to fall in this area than had fallen on the Somme, and this foretold of a large attack to come. Billy would be going over the top. Again. The bombardment was relentless. Men awoke from their haunted slumbers with headaches. The percussion from these large ugly shells was felt in every inch of their worn and tired bodies. It always seemed perverse to Billy that he was forced to endure the most extreme undertakings at a time when his body seemed the most tired. He wondered how different it may be if men who were fully rested, fully fed and fully prepared were used for assaults. It seemed that the need for sleep was ignored and to survive here one must learn to live without adequate amounts of this luxury. This was the theme that united all wars, the complete disregard for the temporary escape of sleep. All great Generals through history experienced this aspect along with their men, Henry V, Napoleon, Alexander the Great, Cromwell. But not this war. Generals were sleeping in comfortable beds in comfortable chateaux. I digress.

Billy's platoon was in the reserve trench awaiting the orders to move forward to the front trench for the attack. They all knew it would be coming soon but none knew exactly when. Only the mid ranking officers and above knew this. The men found dugouts in the trench, Billy with the usual crowd of his section. There was a cursory inspection from a Major none had seen before and then they brewed tea and had rations handed out. All of this was carried out amid the booming sound and tremors of the bombardment that continued unabated around every activity performed. The young and inexperienced among them were visibly shaken by the violence they were living under.

Their Subaltern, 2nd Lieutenant Brown came around later to inspect all equipment. Each man was to have his rifle, sixty rounds, bayonet, four bombs, a dagger and helmet. A selected few were issued wire cutters which hung down from the thigh. These were the weapons they had for the assault on Arras.

For four hours they waited in the reserve trench. The men were quiet as talking would have been futile under such a din. A murmured cheer crept along the line and a corporal appeared to show the reason. Strapped to his body was a large barrel which contained rum, which he generously spooned into the awaiting Infantrymen's tip cups. As he approached Billy, KRP, Johnny and Paulo he offered a grin as each of then dipped the tins into the barrel, filling them to the brim. KRP, now without his customary smile raised his cup and the rest followed. 'To Safety' he shouted making himself heard above the noise. They all touched cups and looked at one another. Fear had conquered them and with shaking hands they consumed the potently strong liquid. The contents of the tin cups were enough to induce intoxication for most men and these were no exception. The brown liquid ran down Billy's cheek as he slurped at his tin cup's contents. Suddenly Billy moved and hugged his three friends, looking for comfort. His actions were reciprocated by them all and they mustered the best smiles they could to each other. The weather had turned much colder and snow was now falling heavily. They all took another large swig just as the order to advance was screamed along the line. They were to move to the front trench and prepare for the attack. Paulo slapped Johnny on the back as the four of them began the journey towards the abyss. They were but a tiny part of the British Army that attacked Arras that day, but it felt to them that they alone when embarking on this supreme test of masculinity.

The guns were yet louder and were falling just a short distance ahead of them onto the German positions. They arrived at the disembarkation point. The ladders were in position and they were to climb in sections, one man at a time. Johnny grabbed the wooden frame, thereby volunteering to be first. He looked at the others as he did so, his face as white as marble with tears in his eyes. The young Officer appeared and went directly to another ladder, pushing the man positioned at its base away. He would be first to go over, he who blew the whistle. The attack was soon, very, very soon.

Suddenly, with deafening impact, the guns ceased. No sound. An incongruous silence. The soft snow flakes fell gently around them and the newly risen sun was hidden by black clouds. Unusual weather for the day after Easter. The silence continued until a voice screamed 'Fix Bayonets'. The assault now imminent, the hearts of over one hundred thousand British and Commonwealth troops beat yet faster.

Billy squeezed the barrel of his rifle and gritted his teeth. He tried to take deep breaths but his shaking prevented him. Just as his legs were about to give way, the eerie shriek of the tin whistles sounded along the line. Johnny climbed the ladder, Billy next, followed by KRP and Paulo. Before Johnny reached the summit the machine gun fire started, evidence that the intense bombardment had not destroyed all before it. He continued his climb, reached the top and was over. Billy followed reached the top and was exposed to the sight of complete desolation. Wire and wood lay everywhere, smoking shell holes as deep as three men lay around and the British were inching forward on the exposed open ground. The snow impeded the view and Billy turned around to see his friends. To his relief, all of them had made it up and all stood crouched down slowly advancing forward. They were implicitly told never to group, yet they were all too close. The machine gun rounds from German positions fizzed past them and explosions tore at the ground around them. They had no idea where the fire was coming from, but began to hear the horrific sound of lead rounds, flying at extreme velocity, hitting cloth and then human flesh. The sound was like a smack, as though a cricket ball had been thrown at a hanging carpet.

These sounds were followed by screams as men witnessed flesh and limbs being removed and flung around the muddy field. The shells were falling more readily. Still they advanced slowly, looking ahead for a suitable shell hole in which to crouch and hide. Finally an officer tried to gain some order amongst the disorganised infantry and through the noise somehow managed to arrange the company in a spaced out line. Men were falling all around now but Billy and his close friends had avoided the thousands of flying bolts of lead fizzing by them. The Captain of the company ordered the men to kneel and fire their rifles on a position ahead which was a tangled mass of wire and wood. The keen eyed commander had noticed that this was where several machine guns were plying their trade. Billy's section obeyed the commands like new schoolboys and within moments volleys of rifle fire destroyed the position taking the numerous machine guns with them.

'Now go' shouted the intrepid commander and they all followed him forward shouting war cries at the awaiting Germans. Shell fire became heavier, heavier German artillery now attempting to slow the British progress. But still they advanced, thousands of khaki clad British, in the open killing fields moving forward.

Two miles behind this action, a young German artilleryman looked around at his comrades loading their 77mm field gun and firing away. The other guns in his battery had adjusted to the new coordinates but still he stumbled over the clumsy handle to lower the angle. His commander eyed him with disdain, conveying an order of 'Get on with it Boy' without moving his lips. But he wanted to get it right, no point firing on his own men.

After more fumbling he finally had the barrel in the right position.

'Klar' he shouted and moved away. The shell was loaded, chamber shut and thick cord pulled. With a flash the 7 kg shell flew from the gun.

Having disabled one position, the British captain looked for the source of more machine gun or rifle fire that was slowing the progress. His muddied face looked up and darted left and right until he saw muzzle flashes and directed his men at them. He stood and pointed and the men stopped and lined up once more. As he stood a rifle round tore into his groin. The violent impact made him spin on his feet as more rounds flew into his upper legs and stomach, rounds emanating from the very positions he had isolated. Billy aimed his rifle at the spot, angered at the presumed death of his company commander. He fired and more fired with him, but less than he expected. He glanced at his side to see far fewer men with him now. Many had fallen, some silent, some screaming like new born babies. This sound blended with screams of rage, exploding artillery, machine guns, rifles, trench mortars and hapless orders, creating a scene of total confusion.

Gravity finally took a grip of the shell and it began its return to earth. Below were thousands of men, some running, some still, and many dead. The shell was surrounded by other shells, flying through the air, dipping their noses as they fell to earth. This shell fell towards a group of British Infantry, closing in on a small section of men firing volleys of rifle fire. One of the group was standing. He had black hair and a large incongruous moustache. The shell was aiming straight for him, but gravity pulled it down, making contact with the ground right between his legs. The percussion fuse was suitably compressed. The shell exploded.

KRP did not see, nor hear this particular shell. Although they were whining through the air and exploding all around, the shell that took his life gave no notice of its impending arrival. He was literally thrown into the air in a perverse cartwheel shape reaching over twenty feet in height. The soldiers close by ducked down, Billy, Paulo and Johnny amongst them. Billy caught the sight of his friend in the air and rushed to the place he would land. The impact of the explosion had killed the man to KRP's left instantly, but he himself lay in the mud crudely cut in half. His legs up to his waist had landed elsewhere and the shell's explosion and its shrapnel had served to remove the lower part of him. Billy was first to him, ignoring the orders of his officer to leave him and continue firing. KRP was alive and looked up at Billy as he held him. Paulo and Johnny tried to get close but the firing of the company prevented them.

KRP was trying to say something but blood had filled his mouth and gave his white teeth a deep crimson outline. He gave out a scream as realisation hit him and Billy held the face of his friend. His stomach was wide open with blood pouring out through his exposed pelvis. The intestines slowly eased out of the large serrated wound spilling onto Billy's hands continuing onto the muddy ground. The eyes in KRP's head turned inwards as though looking above him. With a gut wrenching groan he gave the world his final utterance and the man who had given so much laughter and fun to those around him died. Billy contained his anguish in a restrained but unpreventable groan just as the others from his section arrived. Still rifle and machine gun fire pinged around them all and soldiers were falling and screaming around them. But they were oblivious to all of this; their complete attention was on their friend who was lying mutilated and dead before them. His blood leaked onto the virgin snow which now covered the field. A red slush surrounded them all.

'Keep firing' went the order but they were all frozen and prostrate in their positions. A rifle round ricocheted off the top of Paulo's tin helmet, just denting it but no more. The firing suddenly became fiercer and the officer gave an order to all lie down. This time they obeyed. The remnants of KRP's lower half was scattered around as they resumed their musketry duties. The members of the company now at least knew what they were to do as the German positions were evident. A few more volleys would be enough and a charge of the positions would follow.

The over-riding sentiment of shock was replaced by one of anger and Billy, Paulo and Johnny all wanted to get close to the Germans, to take retribution for the mutilation of their friend. If a charge was ordered, there was no doubt it would be obeyed. As the snow continued to fall, the order was duly given.

There were over a hundred remaining men who took part in the charge. The new commanding officer was another 2nd Lieutenant, standing into the breach created by the fall of the Captain. All as one, they rose and charged the fifty yards towards their enemy's trench line. At first very little fire greeted them, but the reason was soon clear. The Germans had decided upon their own charge at that very moment. Hundreds of clay clad soldiers suddenly began surging towards them. Finally the British had a close and visible enemy to deal with. More courage was mustered from each man as they hurled themselves forward in preparation for a medieval hand to hand clash. The Germans were shouting an indiscernible war cry which raised their own spirits but did nothing to dampen those of Billy and his comrades. They all wanted this fight and cared not what may follow. Some men fired from their hips but the opposing forces were soon so close that the cumbersome rifle was of better use as a spear and the fixed bayonets of each army pointed directly at one another while the distance between them rapidly diminished.

Billy eyed an opponent who eyed him back. He was shorter and older than Billy, but appeared to be shouting orders. The much famed German NCO. Billy's thoughts left Paulo and Johnny and concentrated on this man. Both he and his German pointed bayonets towards each other as they took their final muddy steps. The German was on strong. He thrust his rifle, which was longer than Billy's, but Billy managed to parry it away. The German was very quick and energetic; thrusting from many angles and Billy was on the defensive, only avoiding his opponent's thrusts, not making any of his own. The German was so energetic that Billy was being pushed back, ever fearful of the sharpened blade that was flying close to his face. His footing was unsteady as he tried to take the initiative but his opponent was too fast. Billy felt that this contest could go against him very soon. Billy's rifle was more and more damaged from his defensive blocks and one thrust seemed to go right through his defence, tearing at the tail of his loosened tunic. The German smiled, knowing he was winning. With a shriek of some German phrase he recoiled in preparation for a greater thrust which looked destined to reach its target or smash Billy's defensive tool apart. Suddenly a butt of a rifle flew through the air, connecting with the German's jaw. The impact knocked him clean off his feet and the owner of the rifle jumped towards his fallen prey. It was Paulo. He had saved Billy's life and proceeded to bayonet the stomach of the German again and again. Somewhat cowardly, Billy took his damaged rifle and added his own thrusts into the dead body of his vanquished foe when he saw again, the unmistakable smile of Paulo. His uniform was covered in blood and gore and had evidently been doing some killing prior to moving on to help Billy. With a wink, he moved onto his next hapless victim and he appeared unstoppable. This was another huge surprise as Paulo had never shown such aggression before, but at this moment he was a killing machine seemingly enjoying every minute.

Around them men were engaged in single duals using bayonets and daggers with occasional rifle fire from close range. The British were badly outnumbered and began to move back. Paulo, however, continued going forward and very soon found himself ahead of his comrades. Billy tried to get close but his path was blocked by an enemy with a dagger who had launched himself onto Billy when they both hit the snowy but muddy ground. Billy easily flipped him around and took his own dagger, thrusting it into his throat. His blood sprayed over Billy's face, some in his mouth and Billy was only interested in getting him away to help Paulo who would be dangerously exposed by now.

Billy finally found his feet through the slippery snowy

mud and caught sight of Paulo. He was surrounded by several Germans, one of whom had his arm around his neck and hand over his mouth. The others were busily bayoneting his body and legs, making dozens of insertions and twisting the steeled edge of their blades while inside Paulo's body, hence making as much internal damage as possible. Paulo was screaming at the top of his voice, in Italian. This was another first as he had never used his parents' language before. But there was no way out for him. His injuries already too serious to allow survival. His body suddenly fell limp but still they stabbed away, stabbed and thrusted away at the gallant body of Billy's friend.

Another charge from further Germans obscured Billy's view and the British line broke. Men turned and ran back for the safety of their trench and Billy lost sight of his slaughtered friend. To remain in this area meant certain death and Billy took a step back which resulted in a full scale retreat. Germans were all around now, firing also at the fleeing British. If some order could be restored, the rout could be prevented. Another volley into the ragged ranks of the Germans would halt their advance and he grabbed the nearest British soldier he could and shouted for him to hold firm. To his surprise Johnny joined him along with several others and Billy gave the order to open fire, although he had no working rifle himself. Open fire they did and immediately several Germans close by hit the floor. They fired again and more British joined. Within a few seconds a line of British Infantry had formed and their volleys caused havoc among the cavalier ranks of their adversaries. The British picked their targets and many Germans, unable to form a line of their own, retreated back themselves. The rout had been prevented. As they headed back Billy could see they were dragging the wounded figure of the captain who had led the initial assault. He was alive but very badly injured and would present a huge prize for the Germans. They would extract much useful information from him if they managed to get him back. The British continued firing but led an organised retreat now back to their lines as they were too few to capitalise on the

German retreat. Johnny appeared at Billy's side, out of breath.

'Billy, where's Paulo. Where's Paulo?' he shouted. Billy offered no answer but broke the rank and ran towards the Germans who were taking the captain. They were slow to retreat, hampered by their limp and uncooperative captive. German soldiers were falling all around them but still they did not let go, searching for the award that would surely be theirs for such a prisoner. Billy drew his dagger and lunged towards them. They were both so young and Billy plunged his blade into the back of the first he came to. Rifle rounds were flying around their heads as the hapless German screamed at his wound, dropped the captain and tried to run away, offering no resistance. The Dagger was buried up to its hilt in his back and he fell within a few paces. With no weapon left, Billy threw a swinging right handed punch at the face of the remaining German who also dropped his prey and ran back to his friends who were in full scale retreat. Billy took the wounded captain onto his shoulders and began the long journey back to his trench. The British had retreated back by now and were spilling over the parapet to finally find refuge from this hell. The Germans had similar ideas and Billy managed the journey without being hit. The captain was telling Billy to leave him as the cumbersome journey seemed futile but Billy kept falling and going again. Eventually, when several yards from home, a group of British joined him and pulled the wounded Captain into the safety of the trench and Billy soon followed. The captain, despite his terrible pain, murmured his thanks at Billy, talking of medals and promotions until he finally passed out with the pain. But he was alive. All around the trench were wounded British who had somehow found their way back, along with many fit soldiers who had endured and survived a desperate battle. Billy was completely unharmed, not a scratch on him.

He hastily scanned the trench for Johnny. There was no sight of him and Billy, still buoyed by the war rage that was in him ran the length of the trench shouting for his friend. He asked men as he ran by, nobody answering. He retraced his steps back to the point he had entered, past the unconscious captain but still there was no sight. He again climbed the ladder that was still in position determined to find Johnny, hoping he was lightly wounded in no man's land. As he ascended the ladder he felt arms trying to pull him back, but he was determined. He must find Johnny. He just must. As he clambered over, there was not much firing but that would follow in time. The Germans were probably doing the same as the British; nobody really wanted any more fighting. Billy was then subjected to the awful sight that the recent fighting laid before him. Everywhere were twisted bodies of men. Most were still but some were crawling senselessly in no particular direction. Men wailed in pain from bayonet and rifle wounds and Billy felt alone in a land of the dead and dying, while he wandered through them searching. There were so many dead over such a large area, British and German entangled together. In some places the dead lay on top of each other forming a pile of death. The melted snow around the field became a mush of mud and blood and still Billy, like a ghost walked through this landscape eyes down, examining every body he came to.

Then he saw him. Face down, all limbs in tact, no sign of explosion, no blood. His hopes rose and he dived down. Over a hundred yards away a German watched him over his parapet, rifle in hand. He had Billy in his sights but did not shoot. Not yet, he thought.

Billy was by Johnny's side and he turned him over. What he saw ran through him like a thunderbolt and he jumped like a startled kitten. Johnny's face was unrecognisable on account of a neat bullet wound clean through the middle of his face. The surrounded skin seemed pulled in to the entry wound, like fabric drawn into a pull on a fine silken material. The exit wound was hidden by his helmet, which displayed a hole where the round had flown away after exacting its dreadful damage. It was plain that Johnny was quite dead and must have been hit just moments after Billy had gone to the rescue of the captain. Billy looked to the sky and shouted in his loudest voice. The watching German saw this as too much license and let off a round over Billy's head, as if to tell him that's enough now, get back in. Billy rose to his feet and thrust his chest in the direction where he thought the round came from. 'Shoot me then you Bastards.'

But no shot came and Billy turned and walked slowly away back to his trench. It had happened again. All his friends had been lost. Again.

Billy was in a complete daze after this affair. He was unable to talk to anyone, his mind was in a place it had never been. His feelings were beyond despair, he felt he was at complete boiling point, just ready to explode into an uncontrollable rage at any point. The men were all sent back for roll call which was a pitiful affair. Both sides agreed a brief armistice to collect the dead, but this role fell to one of the pioneer battalions that found employment in this type of work. There were burials for all those recovered, included were Paulo, KRP and Johnny. Billy actually cried at this occasion and threw a pipe into the pit which contained the shrouded bodies of over sixty men. As the pioneers filled the pit Billy remained staring at the newly disturbed earth. He was approached by the new Lieutenant of his platoon, the previous incumbent being covered in a white sheet and residing some eight feet below them. He told Billy that he was to make his way to Battalion head-quarters. They wanted to offer him a commission.

'Yes Sir' Billy replied quietly, not looking up, unable to muster any enthusiasm.

His trip to the headquarters confirmed the promotion and Billy Mercer was to go for Officer training in Gailes in Scotland for ten weeks and be commissioned as a second Lieutenant in another battalion of the Fusiliers. His courage in the recent show and his organisational skills in orchestrating the rifle fire had saved a complete rout and many lives. He had been recommended by many officers, especially the wounded captain whose life he had saved. They told him men had done less and received the VC, but

Billy was recommended for the Military Medal which was duly awarded. These medals meant nothing at all to him; he felt Paulo deserved far more recognition for gallantry than he did.

Chapter 12

It was with a heavy heart that Billy left the front and began his journey to Scotland. He considered that he was abandoning his friends who lay in the ground in a windswept corner of France.

Gailes was no Sandhurst. This officer training school concentrated in field commissions, those of enlisted men, gaining officer status. Billy found many aspects of the whole place rather amusing. They had classes in how to eat at the table (you have to pass the port to the left you know!), how to greet fellow officers even how to dance! This aspect was fun for Billy and his rhythm and ability at this discipline was of a higher standard than the instructors. But these classes were a side show. The men at Gailes were trained in procedure and protocol for British Officers. The duties of a Subaltern were explained, welfare details of troops within a platoon, reporting structure to company and battalion. Infantry tactics were taught, much of which concerned open warfare and therefore had no relevance to the real fighting that was occurring in this war. Examination papers were regularly set, some passed, some not. It was an intensive course yet still rather casual. There was a lot of sport played and it was at Gailes that Billy met and befriended Walter Tulls, a black soldier who was to be commissioned. Billy knew of this man because he played football for Tottenham Hotspur. Billy was no fan of Spurs but was happy to meet Walter and the men became good friends. Everyone was keen on Walter and his colour was not an issue to any potential officer at Gailes. He made the football games a farce as nobody could get the ball off him, so he mostly played the role of referee. When the course was complete, the men went their separate ways, exchanging addresses and promising to meet again after the war. Billy hoped he would see him again but tried to restrain his fondness as everyone he had ever had regard for in the war was killed and he did not want to apply this curse to Walter.

They threw a party on the night they received their commissions and ladies from a well connected families locally were invited. Billy met a very attractive and willing Presbyterian girl whose actions belied her strict religious upbringing. Billy promised to write but lost her address almost as quickly as taking it. The next day he could not remember her name for the life of him. Deirdre? No. Dillys? O never mind!

Back from overseas again. This time a Military transport took him from the Firth directly to Belgium.

His voyage was shared by soldiers from countless Scottish regiments all in different coloured kilts. He had served with these soldiers and held them in very high regard. He would not admit it of course, them being Scottish and all and him from London. Convention had it during his upbringing that anyone from outside of London was an insignificant turd. But the war was changing this perception as many pre existing perceptions had changed during this war. Billy was himself the epitome of this. A lad with his upbringing was now an Officer in the British Army. One brightly polished pip on each shoulder and a personal servant waiting for him on his return. Quite amazing, Billy Mercer now Second Lieutenant Mercer Sir! This realisation brought a smile to his face and he was determined to make the most of his new, privileged rank. He had only achieved it through his performance on the battlefield and the horrors of those experiences deserved respect.

Chapter 13

After another arduous trip lasting almost two days Billy arrived back at the communication trench and proceeded to the officers' mess to meet his colleagues. This section of the line was far neater and better maintained than the muddy bogs he was used to. As he walked along the well constructed duckboards he was regularly met with salutes from worn out soldiers. All had the unmistakable spirit of the British soldier, all stopping in their tracks, standing to the side, strongly saluting and adding a cheerful 'Afternoon Sir'. Billy returned their salutes with politeness and slight awkwardness. He asked a Private for directions to Company headquarters, C Company and was not directed, but led there. Life seemed already easier as an Officer. The head-quarters were hardly that of a Battalion, Brigade or Divisional HQ. This was a large dugout in the side wall of the trench, covered with corrugated iron ceiling. A thick velvet curtain separated the dugout from the trench which was the second line from the front, still only twenty or so yards from No-Man's-Land. The large central room had a table positioned directly in the middle with five non matching chairs around it, one with a leg far shorter than the rest. This table was used for writing, eating and reading orders and maps. To the sides of the room were five metal framed beds, two with curtains which offered some privacy. On the left side was a larger recess which served as the kitchen. The batman, Private Rowland lived, slept and worked here, trying to concoct sensational dishes from rations and parcels which followed Officers around the muddy fields of France and Belgium. Kit and equipment lay everywhere and coat stands held lanterns that gave a misty dull glow to the dusty room. The smell of cigarette smoke and dirty bodies hit him as he entered. There were five officers in this dugout, one Captain, one Lieutenant and three Subalterns of which Billy was one.

When Billy entered the trench there were two other officers present, one, another subaltern, at the table, another, the Captain laying on his bunk reading a letter by the light of a flickering candle.

As his eyes adjusted to the light he could see the bright face of a young man approaching him with his jolly voice and an extended hand to shake. Billy took his hand and whispered in a far less enthusiastic voice. 'Billy, Billy Mercer, nice to meet you.' Billy immediately liked this man. He was always fond of those who gave a large hello and Eddies was most welcoming. Billy noticed that Eddie was a striking looking man, like an actor. Captain Barnes rose from his bed and gave Billy another pleasant greeting. Billy felt he liked this group already. The 8th Battalion RF were, again, his kind of people.

Eddie Tompkin quickly volunteered for the role of taking Billy around to meet his troops and examine this part of the line which was to be his home. As they walked Eddie explained that rumour of Billy and his achievements had reached them all prior to his arrival and this manifested itself into a celebrity status that Billy enjoyed with this Battalion.

Now Eddie had been to Sandhurst. He had all the credentials that a candidate for the Royal Military Academy should. Like his Father, he was educated at Charterhouse School where he was captain of the first XI cricket team. He was a keen member of the Officer Training Corp at school as the country prepared its well educated young men to be leaders for the upcoming war. He was at his last year at school when war was declared, but due to a knee injury he waited a year before joining Sandhurst. His family were so proud as he received his commission, although his Mother was subdued that day. Eddie just followed a path, she thought, nobody ever seemed to ask his opinion. His Father strongly disagreed and felt it imperative that the Tompkin family should have someone at the front as their second son was a cripple and would be unable to serve. Family pride, that's what Mr Tompkin believed, was paramount.

Eddie had been at the front for three months before

Billy's arrival. The largest action he had witnessed was a German assault which the British successfully defended. A bombardment preceded the attack, a bombardment that had killed a number of Eddie's men. The subsequent assault was a terrifying experience. To look over the parapet at thousands of grey clad monsters approaching who want only your death can be unsettling. Some Germans reached the trench but most were cut down in no man's land and Eddie's platoon was responsible for the deaths of many of these men.

When this battle had finished, Eddie had been sick over the trench floor, an act that drew sniggers from his experienced men, who had delighted in the number they had killed.

Eddie had a striking aspect to him. He was the most handsome man. His thick blond hair curled at the front and fell onto his chiselled face. His complexion was darker than most, which blended with hazel striking eyes. He had the look of Michelangelo's David. Of average height with a slim frame he had a voice that was soft and sweet that occasionally sounded like he was singing as he spoke. Since his youth girls and women had given him their full attention, but female attention made him feel shy and awkward. He had a number of sweethearts but he felt that in reality, he had gone along with their desire for him rather than his attraction to them. He was too nice to say no, yet had never met a girl whom he really liked. Since becoming a soldier he had been exposed to the rawness of romance in the army. That is, visiting an institution, getting drunk and taking things from there on a very short lived arrangement. This he liked better.

Eddie was looking forward to meeting Billy. It was testament to the character of Billy Mercer that even those who did not know him, knew of him. People would talk about the big personalities in the trenches and Mercer was one such person of the Royal Fusiliers. He had been party to the papers on the new officer that was to join his battalion and having garnered snippets of information, he took it upon himself to learn more. As it was, Eddie knew all about their new man, making his large and warm welcome unsurprising.

This sector of the line had been active. There were constant whiz bangs at night, lots of sniping and the occasional unprovoked gas or artillery attack.

Billy slowly got used to his position as an officer and slowly got to know his fellow officers, men and duties he needed to perform. He still felt a close affinity to the men and spent many hours chatting to the members of his platoon, more time than most junior officers. The ghosts of his recent past came back to haunt him at night. Occasionally he could smell the smoke from KRPs pipe or hear an Italian accent that could only be Paulo. It was his mind playing with him, but he felt these ghosts would always be with him. They were in the front line trench for a number of weeks and then back further for a number of weeks followed by R and R yet further back. It was at these times that they had the chance to visit local towns where drinking and fucking resumed in abundance. Billy deliberately tried to remain distant to his new group but in time he opened up and let them in, especially Eddie. Eddie was unlike anyone he had met. Where Billy came from, men's emotions were never discussed, as most had none. Billy found himself talking about his friends and the battles he had seen. He conveyed his feeling of emptiness and guilt and was not ridiculed but met with understanding from Eddie. As the months went by, the two of them became closer, keeping each other's company above all else's. They enjoyed many drunken sessions and Billy enjoyed hunting women with Eddie as his fantastic looks made it far easier to approach any women he chose. During this time Billy would try to charm the French women who gathered around British Officers. These were the most attractive and dignified, whose own lives had been somewhat disturbed and impoverished by the fighting in France. Many were struggling to live with their husbands away or dead and played the roles of courtesans to make ends meet. No money would change hands but the expectation was that the unsuspecting officer would fall in love and shower them with gifts and opportunities to meet higher ranking, more influential men. Billy and Eddie were happy to play the initial part of the game, but failed to play the second and in the process enjoyed some of the most amazing sex. These women were drawn to Eddie's looks and Billy's humour made them a formidable pair. On one occasion Billy became intimate with the known lover of a Colonel from the artillery. The Colonel sent an envoi to request Billy not see her again. Billy refused, not from regard for the tart, merely to agitate a senior Officer. He met her subsequently at a bombed chateau and noticed the same Colonel sitting in his car outside, with reddened eyes, surveying the scene as Billy walked out of the house with a satisfied look. As he passed the staff car he puckered his lips and blew a kiss to the hapless Colonel, laughing as he walked away. Silly old sod, he thought.

As the weather turned colder it was becoming apparent that this sector was hotting up. There was more sniping and indiscriminate shelling. Many men were being killed and wounded by small skirmishes, trench raids and improvised explosive devices. Men were also falling ill from fever and some injuries sustained in the sector came from suspicious sources. Sentry duties were increased and a full sense of alertness pervaded the sector. Men were sent out at night to repair wire or watch the enemy and this precarious exercise brought increasing casualties. Eddie's platoon had lost almost a third of their strength and new, young replacements were regularly filling the ranks. Lieutenant Parker from 2 platoon was killed while on a reconnaissance mission and was replaced by a young subaltern who looked hardly eighteen. Billy took the diffident figure of Lieutenant Turner around explaining life in the sector. He was going soft, he thought, but he was starting to feel more and more pity for the young soldiers and officers alike who were thrown into the front with little training or understanding of what to do.

Billy was on his bed with a large bottle of whisky, which was emptying more rapidly as each moment passed. Eddie was at the table with a glass full of whisky writing a letter to the family of a boy who was killed within three days of joining the platoon.

'Your son was a fine soldier who died a noble death fighting for the protection of the country that was so dear to him. He will be sorely missed by all who knew him.' He scribbled the words he had written so many times before, knowing they would offer little solace to an unsuspecting family in England.

'Noble death? Noble death? How many men have you seen experience a noble death Billy?'

Billy half looked, half grinned and continued swigging his Scotch while eyeing the corrugated iron that formed the roof of the dugout.

'There are no noble deaths here. A noble death is one in which an old man lies in a clean bed surrounded by grandchildren and a million wonderful memories with a deep final breath.'

His voice was getting louder, the grip on his glass stronger, the look in his eyes sterner.

'All we see are men not twenty, screaming to their pitiful deaths without a compliment of limbs or blown to the four winds with only enough left to fill a fucking sandbag!' His voice had reached a crescendo with those final words as he threw his glass against the muddy wall of the dugout not even managing to break it.

'I don't know how I can carry on writing this shit!'

Billy swigged again, enjoying the pungent smell of the whisky and with a half glance casually rose from his bed and stepped out of the dugout to inspect some new troops which had just arrived. How long before he'd be writing similar letters to their families. About a week in his experience.

Billy was due some leave. He would be going home to visit his mother who he had heard was unwell. The correspondence between him and his Mother had dried up. He could not bring himself to answer her letters and after a while she stopped writing. He would put that right when he saw her. He would explain his difficulties, tell her about Eddie, his new rank and dispel some ideas that he knew were held back home. He would be allowed six days leave and intended to take some of his wine booty home, sell it and give his mother the proceeds and ensure that she bought something nice. Eddie went with him one balmy evening and with the map in hand, they travelled the ten miles or so to where the treasure was buried and dug up several cases. He gave two bottles to Eddie and they drunk two on their return. The sale of the remainder should bring enough for Billy's mother to buy a complete set of new furniture, some nice clothes and shoes. He was looking forward to seeing her face. When they returned to the reserve trench a letter was waiting on the table. It was in the handwriting of his Aunt. His heart sank. Reluctantly he opened the letter which told him all he had feared. His mother's illness had deteriorated and she had contracted pneumonia. A week ago his mother had succumbed and died.

Billy left the dugout on reading those words. He went straight to Battalion headquarters and cancelled his leave. He had no reason to return to London. He would stay in France.

For a week he could hardly speak, but Eddie understood and left him until he was ready to talk. Eventually he did and fighting tears he explained his guilt and devastation. While the guns sounded outside the dugout and explosions blew dust into the dugout, Eddie held him and comforted him. Billy could get through it with the help of his friend. The bombardment stopped and Billy slept under the watchful eye of his friend.

Chapter 14

Billy was awoken by the sound of machine gun fire from the German lines. This could be the precursor for an attack. Billy, Eddie and young Turner ran out of their dugout gathering their men to man the steps in preparation. Billy looked through the periscope as men climbed to man the machine guns while others loaded trench mortars. It was just before dusk, a good time to attack. Billy peered left and right but found no Germans approaching. How strange, he thought. He looked back at his men. Practically the whole company were out of their dugouts, on the fire-steps of the trench and this arrangement was emulated along the entire line for as far as one could see. He was confused as suddenly from the distance he heard the sound of rumbling of hundreds of guns from behind the German lines. He looked to the East and saw numerous spotter balloons miles back from the lines. With a sinking heart, Billy realised what was happening. This was a trap.

'Back in Dugouts. Get Back' He yelled for all he was worth. Everybody looked with confused faces but as the shells approached they realised one by one. The machine gun fire was to draw them out of the dugouts while an artillery barrage with shrapnel shells was aimed at the soldiers. Before they had moved a few paces the shells began to land. A number fell just in front of the trench, a number behind, but many plopped directly into the trench, on top of the infantry, exploding as they hit. The effect was devastating. The roar of the approaching shells mixed with the din of the explosions and wood and earth and wire and bodies flew into the sky. The trench walls were rapidly diminishing under the impact of the explosions and men were being killed in dozens with every direct hit. The men tried to orientate themselves and find their way back to the protection of a dugout, climbing over a detritus of ripped and torn bodies. Blood was along the walls and floor of the trench as Billy ran the length to find protection of his dugout. He pulled as many man as he could into the second line where his protection was situated, but the boundaries of one trench and another were being blown apart. Shrapnel flew everywhere and men crouched down on the base of the trench for protection, but still the shells fell. It was living in the epicentre of an earthquake, the ground rumbled below them and the noise was enough to deafen a man. Shrieks of agony and wails of fear almost matched the sound of explosions and men were buried where they stood by tonnes of falling, recently disturbed earth. In the confusion Billy caught sight of Eddie, lying on the floor of the trench with his arms around his head whining like a violinist playing just the E string. Men ran this way and that, desperately seeking shelter, while being turned to dust by direct explosions feet away. He grabbed Eddie's prostrate frame by his Sam Browne strapping and dragged him into the Officers dugout. Many men had already occupied this stronger recess and man lay on one another keeping out of the storm. Shells fell all around them, the impact taking their breath away. The iron roof offered protection from flying objects and shrapnel but a direct hit would have done for them all.

This was a well planned and accurate artillery assault. Not far from Billy's mind was the possibility that this was a harbinger of an infantry attack and no man he was close to seemed particularly well prepared to defend their lines from waves of approaching German infantry.

They lay in the dugout, plotting the progress of every approaching shell in their minds. Was this the one? The next one?

Men were terrified, crouching in foetal positions or trying to bury themselves into the earth like a mole to escape the rain, hoping the barrage would stop. But the barrage did not let up. They stayed in this position for almost five hours, but the direct hit never came. The dugout was badly damaged, holes perforated the iron roof and walls had partially collapsed but after this duration the shellfire became less frequent and eventually ceased. This was the time the Germans would advance. At the very time that men would collapse with relief or take stock of who had survived the metallic storm, every man was ordered back onto his feet, back to what remained of the front line trench to defend the expected attack. This was no easy task and many men gave every impression they would rather run away than expose themselves to further horror and potential death. But stand they did, as British soldiers do and it is for reasons like this that young officers loved their men and respect for men of all classes grew during this conflict.

There was no fire-step to man on the trench wall. Men now lay on a mound of earth which took the place of the parapet. Debris and pieces of human beings lay everywhere. Wounded men screamed in pain and torsos, heads, arms clothing and blood lay everywhere. Much of the equipment was destroyed by the bombardment, but some machine guns were found along the line and hastily prepared to oppose the onslaught that would surely follow. Billy was ordering men into position with Sergeant Robbins using threats to ensure orders were followed. Billy disliked Robbins but he was effective in getting the job done. The other officers were slowly clearing their heads and organising their men. All except Eddie, who was nowhere to be seen. Billy was in panic over his disappearance. Was he blown to pieces with so many others? Billy was sure he saw him in the dugout and went directly back to check on his friend. On the outside of the dugout were the mutilated corpses of several men, pouring blood into a pool that ran into an indentation on the side of the trench. There, beneath them was Eddie.

Billy hastily pulled back the dead men to expose his friend who was covered in blood. Eddie looked up at Billy. He was alive! His entire body was shaking like a naked man lying in a snowy field.

'Eddie, Eddie,' screamed Billy as he knelt to his side.

'I'm alright. I'm alright. Leave me Billy. Let me lie here.'

Billy realised he was not hurt, not physically hurt, but in his own world of horror.

Billy did as he asked. He left him and went back to his men.

He ran over dead men to return to the fire positions, expecting the assault to have started. But it had not, and it did not. The attack never came. Perhaps the Germans were advancing elsewhere but no machine gun fire was heard.

The observation balloons still hung in the air. They would have learned a lot from this episode and were successful in killing many men. Billy's and Eddie's company of one hundred and thirty men suffered casualties of twenty five killed, forty wounded and twelve unaccounted for. The Captain was killed.

After a further two hours of manning the front line the men were stood down. The attack was not coming. Within hours pioneers came to collect the dead and repair the trenches. The men were relieved back to the reserve trench. It had been a terrifying day.

Chapter 15

It was an ordeal that had to be experienced to be believed. How could anyone at home possibly understand the range of emotions that come with being under such a bombardment? But the attack did not happen. It was a feint. The Germans were testing the British, making them believe an assault was coming. No doubt they were watching from above at the reaction of the British to an assumed attack. The Germans were testing various parts of the line to probe for weakness. This part had held well.

A week passed after such violent activity, with no incident at all, not even a trench mortar. It was considered that the sector was now quiet and leave was issued. Leave was granted for Eddie. Five days at home. Eddie went to battalion HQ to collect his warrant and pleaded the case for Billy to be allowed some time. After drawn out deliberations and explanations it was agreed that Billy could join him. Eddie was elated inside but showed nothing.

Eddie invited him to join him at his home in Hertfordshire. Billy agreed without a great deal of enthusiasm, but they set off together as though going on Holiday, taking some bottles of whisky for the journey and some bottles of wine as a gift to the Tompkins. They were drunk before reaching Calais and made the very most of their provisions and spare time on the journey. When they finally alighted the train at Waterloo, Eddie's family were there to meet him. Eddie had been quiet for the last twenty minutes of the journey, he was anxious about seeing his family again. He felt so distant towards them but wanted to be close, wanted to hug his mother. As the smoke cleared on the crowded platform, the two young Officers presented an attractive sight. They looked straight into the eyes of the awaiting family, Eddie's Father, Mother and younger brother who Billy noticed seemed crippled and deformed in some way. For a moment the son stared frozen in time looking at a family he no longer knew. All members of his family restrained themselves, wanting to run up to Eddie and hug him but feeling this would not be pertinent. This moment lasted less than seconds but seemed to last an eternity. Eddie broke the deadlock finally with a smile, thereby inviting them forward.

They greeted, hugged shook hands and shared a train to Hertfordshire. They arrived in the late evening, changed their clothes and after a while Billy and Eddie adjourned to the local pub, where they drank as much as they could and rudely endeavoured to make acquaintance with almost every girl in the pub, whether accompanied or not. People from the village knew Eddie and while they made efforts to greet him, buy him drinks and pat him on the back, the response they received was not as they expected. They saw a surly and somewhat aggressive young man who seemed to mock them with his cursory one word answers. After a while most left the two alone as they drank into the night, returning home when everyone else had been asleep for some time. The following evening there was to be a dinner thrown in Eddie's favour with a few local friends invited. Mrs Tompkin laid on a lovely meal and they wore their uniforms for the sake of his family and guests. Two couples attended, neither were Eddie's friends, but his Father's. Mr Walsh, a rotund balding man and his attractive, shy and beautifully dressed wife. The other couple were older and particularly uninteresting. Mrs Tompkin realised her choice of guests was a mistake. They all seemed interested in the boys and asked many questions during drinks, but were met with a similar response as the locals in the pub and again it was not long until they realised conversations with them were futile. Billy was seated opposite Mrs Walsh, who he had been gazing at during drinks. She had caught his eye on a number of occasions and Billy wondered whether he was in there.

He looked with raised questioning eyes at Eddie who knew what was happening in his mind. Not wishing to insult his most welcoming guests, this was his way of gaining a form of permission. Eddie was happy for him to give it a try, he'd considered it himself, but it was mainly a fine way of fucking her husband as well, a man he despised more than most, including some generals. He was from the same school and carried all the ignorant self delusions that were continuing to send thousands to their deaths every day. With a nod and lips thrust forward, eyes wide, he was allowing Billy to do what he knew he could, quite easily. Billy smiled, Eddie laughed, the bond between these two men was something quite unusual, but Billy liked it. He loved this man as much as any of his past friends whom he knew for far longer. How he wished they could both get through this and live as close friends forever.

'What's funny?' enquired Mr Tompkin.

'Everything' his son replied, the table ignoring his response as more blurb from a soul they no longer understood.

Billy's eyes turned again to Mrs Walsh. Really quite attractive, her figure was wonderful, those lovely legs just a little too easy to notice. He kept her gaze for a second until she was compelled to turn away, only to return immediately, hoping this young soldier was thinking what he indeed was. She managed as much as a smile that her modesty would allow, but it was enough, the game was afoot. Douglas had noticed the exchanges, he never took his eyes from the brother he admired, Billy gave him a wink, he felt included in this mischievous enterprise.

Eddie was irritatingly playing with a silver salt cellar, spinning it in his fingers and tapping the table with the minute spout. His eyes were focussed on this activity as he slumped back into his chair. Billy noticed him and paid close attention. He had seen this kind of behaviour before.

'Don't do that dear' his mother plaintively requested. Mrs Tompkin was met with just a look from Eddie as he continued. Billy was now concerned, he tried to catch his eye, at which point the bellowing sound of Mr Walsh's voice dominated the table.

'It is perfectly obvious that Germany is practically finished and yet we still do not attack.

A simple artillery barrage and a big push will be enough. The Germans are all de-motivated cowards as these boys here must know. Just bloody well get on with it.'

Eddie raised his eyes from his distraction into Billy's, frowning as he did. They both knew what the other was thinking but his comments did not even warrant replies, so nonsensical did they seem. Then the old fool began to illustrate his points with waving arms, becoming more animated as he did.

'Sweep them out of France. Sweep them back to Germany, Sweep....'

His hand made contact with a wine glass, spilling its contents over the table with the size of stain flattering the volume spilt. It made a crash as it fell but inside Eddie's head it created an explosion. As the wine fell, his mind took him to a place where a man's head was hit with shrapnel and its contents spilled over a dugout in a similar way. The boy's eyes were looking directly at Eddie and all around went quiet because Eddie's consciousness was elsewhere. His nerves then totally, completely and utterly gave way. As a man in an electric chair, he shook losing control of all functions. Billy noticed it first while the others continued to listen to Walsh and the servants cleared the spilt wine.

Eddie stared at the spillage, seeing not wine but blood and brains and the sound of the salt cellar falling violently onto the china plates drew the other guests' attention. A groan escaped from Eddie's mouth as he tried to contain himself without success. This was a most confusing spectacle for the others and immediately Mrs Tompkins leapt to her feet and darted to her son.

'What on earth is wrong with him' spitted Walsh, perturbed by the interruption to his profound utterances.

Billy also rushed around the table and took his friends arms in his hand.

'He's alright Mrs Tompkins, he'll be alright in a moment.'

Still Eddie shook in violent sudden jolts as Billy pushed down his head to prevent it tipping back and endangering his tongue. The entire table looked on in disbelief as Mr Tompkins shouted 'Edward! Edward! Are you alright son?'

They crowded around him until Eddie regained some control while in Billy's restraining arms. He looked at his friend, foaming from the mouth with tears in his eyes and a pained and pitiful expression on his face. He slowly nodded and Billy let go. Eddie immediately found his feet and rushed from the room, the sound of his heavy footsteps up the stairs the only sound.

The room was in shock, all looking at Billy for an explanation. He realised he had an obligation to speak.

'It comes back to us all sometimes. It's usually something stupid that triggers it.' He looked at Walsh. 'He'll be just fine in a moment, we see it all the time over there. It's a reaction of the nerves'.

The meal was first class despite Mr Walsh's constant nonsense. Eddie had recovered himself but remained upstairs while Billy retired with the Gentleman for brandy and cigars but only contributed to conversations with bland one word answers. He could not understand how such a nice man as Mr Tompkin would befriend such a fool as Walsh. He guessed at some dingy financial consideration that behoved him to this irritating man. As he left the drawing room with his generous brandy he caught sight of Mrs Walsh as she crossed the hall, heading for the kitchen, he followed. She was holding a glass of wine which was hardly touched.

'Drink up' Billy impertinently ventured, she started and turned to realise she was at last alone with him.

'I don't like it really', she was relaxed and clearly welcomed the exchange.

Billy started work. He looked her smack in the eyes standing just feet from her, she did not move.

'Maybe it needs more time to mature; perhaps it was opened too early,'

'Perhaps' she replied with an inquisitive look.

'I should think if you came down here at 3 O'clock, you would like the taste of it'

She was exasperated by the comment, how dare he, but how she loved it. Turning instantly red, she merely repeated 'perhaps' and left the kitchen, feeling instantly aroused. Utterly in shock she made her way back to the company. Billy followed directly after her.

He had finished his second large brandy on his own when he heard the creaking of the stairs. It was difficult for him to get drunk now, so used to it his body was. Eddie was the same. That evening they had drunk three or four glasses to each of those drunk by Eddie's father and the pestilent Mr Walsh although the latter was so intoxicated that they all had to carry him up. Dear O Dear O Dear!!

His need for sleep rose in inverse proportions to his resistance to alcohol, his tortured mind could not rest for more that an hour or two, his body had become used to making do with this amount as it was all he managed to get while in the trenches. This was the hardest part to get used to but once mastered, coping with little sleep was a useful accolade as there was so much to do in France sleep seemed like a waste. Eddie was the same. So strange you would think. When you at last had the chance to sleep, you in fact sleep less than you would at the front. They knew the reasons but could not possibly explain.

She appeared as if by clock work. Without a word he approached her tentative nervous face. With a hand on each of her cheeks he pulled her mouth towards his and entered with his tongue. She responded with vigour, exploring all parts of the youth's mouth, unable to resist whatever this young warrior demanded of her. This was sex, not some boring fart but one who had a million volts of life buzzing through every cell of his body, being a man her pathetic husband could never be despite being over twice his age. For Billy the passion was more aggressive. He pulled away and twisted her around so her hands fell on the chopping board on which she was leaning, leaving her back facing him. He immediately put his hands up her dress, pulling away all underclothes, lifting it all up to reveal her bare buttocks.

She could not stop it the passion too intense as within a moment he had entered her wet welcoming body and he started to thrust almost with disdain. Within a minute she had reached the powerful climax now wanting to feel his warmth explode into her.

Having satisfied himself he withdrew, leaving the degraded women lying over the block. She could not move out of shame and exhaustion. He leaned down and kissed her bare neck. 'You old romantic you', he thought to himself. Doing up his trousers he left the room. I fancy a walk he thought.

He left the house walking into a thin darkness with the dawn just a few hours away. The night was unusually warm as he headed towards a large oak situated a quarter mile from the house. As he approached he saw the outline of a person, a person he immediately knew to be Eddie.

'Stand Easy' he called. Eddie gave the croaky grunt of a man in tears. Billy understood he was in another dark dark moment. Billy sat at the foot of the trunk, leaving his friend gazing in the distance. 'I just get so fucking scared sometime, as though I cannot possibly go back, I must try to get out of it.' But go back they must, on the 4.35 train tomorrow.

'You'll be alright in the morning mate. I fucked that Walsh woman by the way'

'Oh yes, any good?'

'Yeah, not bad, not at all bad'

Breakfast was an awkward affair, Mrs Walsh boldly holding his gaze, having evidently derived no insult from the previous night's activity, she was even quite proud of herself. No it was not awkward for them, it was awkward for Eddie who dearly wanted to be able to talk to his parents before going back to the Front. But he felt so alien now. He knew the distance was all his doing but he couldn't prevent it.

'Grand to meet you Lieutenant, we hope to see a lot of you.' Eddie's Father warmly said.

'Thank you for a delightful weekend Mr Tompkin, I'm truly grateful to you.'

'Well look after my boy, young man', he took his hand and piercing in his eyes repeated 'look after my boy.'

'Dougieeee, look after yourself matey, keep away from dirty women'.

The young lad chuckled and wanted to say more but needed to give his time to his dear brother.

As Billy walked to the awaiting car, he left his friend with his family and watched them say their final goodbyes through the window. A lovely family he thought. Eddie seemed to have broken the self imposed barrier and hugged each member for a good while. His mother was weeping to see her son go again, his Father dignified as ever, his doting brother nothing but excruciatingly proud.

When finished Eddie almost ran to the car and jumped into the seat next to Billy.

'Right, lets get back to where we belong.'

Chapter 16

When the two officers arrived back at the front line, there was much activity in their sector as several senior officers came out from the officers dugout to which the young subalterns were heading.

'Ah Mercer and Tompkins, there you are, come in a moment, we have something to discuss.'

It was an ominous greeting for them to return to after a long and pleasant leave.

Major Blake was another old style pre war officer. With much unnecessary formality he explained that a trench raid was required somewhere along this line. They had experienced much activity in the German lines ahead of them and wanted to find out what was happening. The Royal Flying Corps had photographs of huge troop and hardware movements, which were a concern for the whole division. The General wanted some prisoners taken and interrogated using whichever means were necessary to learn more of the enemy intentions ahead of them.

'We are honoured that our Battalion has been chosen as we have shown so much fighting spirit in this area. We are looking for an aggressive raid, taking up to a dozen prisoners, some officers if possible. It's a little unfortunate that you boys are in such a contentious section here where I know there is a lot of activity but this company have the men for the job. I think we will need a full company for this one, at least eighty soldiers.'

The Major cleared some cups from the table and spread out a neat and newly written map showing British and German positions.

'I believe that, if we catch them unaware, we could gain control of their forward trench for some time before Hun reinforcements arrive. I want you to kill as many as you can to scare the life out of your prisoners and make them glad they are taken. They'll cooperate more that way. Scour the trench along here for any paperwork which may contain information and we believe the Officers dugout is here.' He pointed to a recess in his neat map. 'Charge in there in some force, shoot a few, grab some and then get them back here like wild fire.' The Major paused and eyed the two. 'This is not straightforward, I do know that lads, but the General himself has said there would be decorations for this one if you are successful.' There was a time when this would mean something, especially to Eddie, but the importance of medals had slowly drained away along with the blood of so many English men.

More details were explained, but this was a very rude welcome for them both. Eddie became visibly nervous as the complacent Major discussed the assault in the fashion of one explaining the arrangements for a Sunday excursion.

There would be four second Lieutenants taking part, but no Captain or Major. They would be in the trench awaiting the prisoners.

There were many trench raids recently and Billy and Eddie had been on the receiving end of a few, losing some men in the process. Neither had taken part in one and this would be a very difficult one to open an account with. The German line was some two hundred and fifty yards away, through shell holes, wire and thick boggy mud. The weather was cold but the constant shelling around this line had churned no man's into a bog. The operation would take some hours and would be preceded by a ninety minute bombardment. Casualties would be high, there was no doubt and there was no guarantee of success at all.

The two other Subalterns were equally concerned. The chances of success were slim and it was only Billy who retained some element of optimism. He relished the idea of having a go at the Boche, he wanted to kill as many as he could at every chance he had. However, the artillery bombardment that he and Eddie endured just prior to their leave had a profound effect on Eddie and Billy knew it. Young Turner, just eighteen gave every impression of being sanguine but this thin veneer was painfully transparent. The fourth Subaltern said not a word but his mind seemed to have gone long before and he looked far older than his twenty eight years. This was a man who seemed resigned to death and this little show could have provided it for him. So, this was the team that would lead the trench raid on the following evening.

The Major wished them all good luck and told them they would be going over at 7.30 pm by which time it would be totally dark and they must get back before day break. Above all they must not allow themselves to be taken as prisoners.

There was little chance for contemplation as they both had duties to perform and it was not until 4am that they returned to their dugout to catch some sleep. The other two subalterns and the captain were out at this time leaving just Billy and Eddie in the dugout. They both took a large few swigs of whisky before falling on their beds. Billy was straight asleep, but Eddie could not. He laid there in the darkened, cold dugout fully clothed. He thought about the following day and he thought about his family. After some time of restlessness he rose to the desk and wrote a long letter home, explaining that he was sorry that he was distant and when the war was over he would explain all. By breakfast time Billy was awake again and they enjoyed their food before both heading to their respective platoons to brief them on the night's work.

The bombardment was to start at six o'clock. With the men fully briefed, all four officers prepared themselves in the dugout. They blacked their faces with charcoal from the fire mixed with grease. Billy loaded his pistol and took his dagger which could see employment this night, but this affair would also be undertaken with bombs. Each man was to carry four and they would try to bomb their way into the German trench. The men would be carrying no equipment with them. They would be light and quick as they performed this task. Each man had an army issue dagger.

Sergeant Robbins entered the dugout.

'A quick word sir.'

Billy looked up and beckoned the irascible Robbins in.

'Some of the men have the wind up a bit, so I've given them a bit of stick sir. Think I've broken Walker's nose, but the little bastard can still go over.'

'What are you doing Robbins, you really are a useless bag of shit. I don't want him coming with us in that condition. He'll be slow and not up to the job. Send him back down the line to get it patched up.'

'I disagree sir, he can't get out of it by being a coward.'

'I don't care what you think Robbins. You have managed to get him out of this. Now get out and get the men ready and no more of that.' Billy continued his tirade at Robbins while the other officers made their silent preparations.

Robbins did not move but stood his ground with his eyes directly into Billy's.

'I told you to get out.' He finally moved away.

'And Robbins.' The Sergeant turned around. 'One day I'll break your bloody nose.'

'Think you could do that do you sir?' Robbins spoke with a smile across his face.

'You should try that one day.' He continued. Billy walked towards him taking up the challenge.

'Leave it Bill, leave him. Sergeant, get back to your work.' Eddie exclaimed. Robbins took the opportunity to leave.

'I do hate that dick,' Billy said as he sat back down to continue his work.

As they continued, Billy noticed all the other Subaltern's hands shaking as they attempted to load rounds into their .455 Webley revolvers. Billy went around them all performing the task for them, without a word being said. As he handed back the last revolver, the bombardment started, loud and powerful, shaking the ground around them. They finished their preparations, put on their tin helmets and left the dugout, for perhaps the last time, to get the men in position ready for the raid. Eddie reached for Billy's shoulder whispering to his friend.

'Good luck old boy. Good luck.'

'You too Eddie, we'll be alright just you see.'

Billy had gone over the top before. Whether it was a small raid or a large assault, it made little difference. The concept of leaving relative safety to enter an arena which would seem to bring only the threat of imminent death was one that worked like madness to a sane mind. The shells which flew over their heads landed hundreds of yards ahead of them but each one shook the ground and the men themselves as the individual explosions amalgamated into one roaring noise which was so violent that men crouched down their heads in the erroneous belief that this would reduce the impact.

The Sergeants called for the ladders which were brought up from the stores in the reserve trench. The voices were inaudible but the order was understood as the ladders were placed against the muddy wall of the trench. Men faced forward, all aware of the task ahead, occasionally looking around at their officers who stood a few paces back. Billy could not see Eddie, who was in an adjacent trench which zigzagged along the line. The next time they would see each other would be in no man's land.

The watches on the wrists of the subalterns laboured to their destination as the officers raised their arms, not utilising the whistles as they wanted some surprise which was surely lost by the artillery. A small drizzle of cold spring rain began to fall as the artillery bombardment stopped as suddenly as it started. The officer's arms swiftly lowered as they stepped forward and were the first to leave their trenches. The men carried rifles with their bombs, daggers in their webbing and soon all then men were above ground. The men could see nothing but darkness ahead of them but were relieved that no enemy fire was coming their way. Billy turned to see that his men were safely over and then sought the sight of his friend who quickly appeared to his right and gazed at Billy for comfort. Then all the men advanced together as one, Billy and Eddie eager to get closer to one another but military procedure would not allow them to bunch up too much. Backs bent, they advanced on their way towards the German line. In the air was the heavy smell of cordite and the smoke from the exploded shell drifted in no man's land towards them.

Still there was no reaction from the Germans to the presence of their enemy in no man's land coming towards them. It was quiet. The ground made for difficult progress as men climbed in and out of shell holes advancing while the Germans ahead finally decided that the bombardment had stopped and took their positions back in their front line. They made good progress, all pleasantly surprised by the lack of German response. At last the first of the German mortars were set up and started their work with the first few shells falling far beyond the advancing men. Half of the distance had now been covered but the Germans now knew of the appearance of the Fusiliers and it would not be long before flares were launched and the machine gun fire would soon follow. Billy turned again to see his friend who was some way behind him now. 'Don't bunch boys, keep going, doing well.'

Another mortar round fell behind them momentarily illuminating them all. Billy held his arm to motion to Eddie who returned the gesture, fear showing in his face. The remaining two platoons seemed to drift towards Billy as the formation began to break up. As Billy looked around the first flare fizzed into the sky, exploding and laying light on the entire field below. More flares reached for the sky and as daylight returned Billy could see the company in its entirety lunging forward. The flares began their slowed return to land and the familiar sound of the first machine gun started when Billy, who was furthest ahead and no further than sixty yards from the enemy trench, fell forward for cover. The remaining men followed. He was ever closer to Eddie now as they both naturally converged on towards each other to gain some welcome company with whom to share this ordeal. The flares, although exposing the raiders' position, also served to show the way through the wire to the German trench. Thankfully the wire at this sector was not too thick and that which was before them had been well damaged by the artillery.

There were several places to pass through but all were fifty yards ahead. Now that they were visible, every soldier knew that the mortars would be more accurate and the machine gun and rifle fire would soon come closer. By now some of the soldiers had found shell holes for cover but if they could advance close to the wire they would be in range for the Mills bombs they all carried. The Germans had been slow but methodical with their duties since the flares went up and the first of the accurate mortar rounds fell on the British positions. The rifle and machine gun fire continued but their effect was not known in the night air. The soldiers continued their advance, one hand on their helmets awaiting orders as shells began to fall among them. A high pitched scream met the explosion of one such round which landed cleanly in the middle of a group from Eddie's platoon. One soldier was blown to pieces, two more were seriously hurt with one losing a leg which lay perfectly severed just yards from its unfortunate previous owner, lit by the eerie greenness from the flares. More flares were launched as more shells fell around and it seemed the Germans knew exactly where they were. The officers back in the British trenches peered over at proceedings through the safety of a periscope, shooting concerned glances at one another over the progress of this operation.

'If this is not well lead, we could see a disaster here' one opined for it was clear the boys were pinned down.

Billy understood that he needed some covering rifle fire to allow for a dash forward to start some bombing. He ordered his platoon down while he crept back and to his right to a shell hole which Eddie, along with his dead and wounded soldiers occupied. The noise was too great to allow conversation, the machine guns, two Billy thought, were now firmly fixed at the top of the shell holes. However, it appeared that the platoon on the far left, that of young Mr Turner had not been seen by the enemy, but were all down seeking cover. Billy managed to crawl to Eddie's hole without injury and grabbed his friend who had not noticed his arrival, having his head pressed firmly into the wall of the shell hole. Billy reached a hand over, grabbing his muddy shoulder and shouting at him from so close that his lips touched Eddie's ear.

'Ed, if I can get Turner to pour some fire on those fucking machine guns, we can all charge up to the wire and get the bombs going. You alright with that?'

Eddie did not answer, but looked at his friend with wide, wild eyes. Bright tracer fire from machine guns bounced around them as Billy waited for some response from Eddie. He was unfortunately in no state to give orders to his men. Billy violently grabbed a soldier and shouted his order for him to cross to the next shell hole and inform Lt Turner to creep to the top of his shell hole with his entire platoon and open fire on the German line. There would not have been more than a platoon or two facing them with two machine guns. If cover fire could keep them pinned down, this should give enough time for the other three platoons to get close enough to use their Mills bombs.

In a rare lull the private looked back at Billy shouting, 'No problem sir, I'll do it. I'll tell them to follow you up immediately you're in aye Sir?'

'Yep, you do that. Like your style fella.' This produced a proud smile on the young soldiers face as he began his crawl out of the back of the ditch that was the small shell hole they occupied.

The young soldier performed his duty well and within a short time the men of 3 platoon started their work as thirty rifles answered the German guns with effective accuracy. The machine gun stopped for a moment as more flares exploded in the sky, now acting as agents for the British more than the Germans as the advancing men at least knew of the whereabouts of their objective. This was what Billy wanted and he rose to his feet with his platoon following. The shade produced by the flares almost protected them because the shadows moved like black devil soldiers joining in the assault. Eddie was some time in mustering his men, half his group charging before he did.

Whatever had happened to Gilbert's platoon was a mystery, the last Billy had seen of them was on his left. It was most likely that they were all taking cover.

The rain was heavier now making the ground more slippery. Billy and his men charged with all the energy they could use, throwing the bombs as they went. The explosions created were modest in comparison to the mortar rounds still falling behind them. As they continued their run, one of Billy's men dropped his bomb, stopping to attempt to find it in the darkness. Men behind him were obstructed by the stationary soldier, standing as he was before the wire when the bomb exploded amongst them, killing he who had dropped it and maiming another. The others ran around this scene, finding gaps in the wire, wanting to stay and help, but fear forcing them forward.

Startled Germans in the trench caught sight of the approaching enemy with Billy leading a group of wild savages towards them. The few rifles opened on them hitting boys behind Billy with a thud, none hitting him. Billy now had revolver in hand, men behind with bayonets on rifles. Just yards from the trench now Billy's men roared like lions firing as they went. A machine gun to their right turned on them, spraying bullets all around them and would have done more damage, had they not been close enough to dive for the trench. For three of his men the trench was not close enough as the stinging lead bullets perforated their bodies and cries of pain and horror of those around them filled the dark and rainy night. For the first time Billy entered a German trench and his gallant men followed.

Five of Billy's rounds in his revolver had been released towards the awaiting Germans, by the time his boys entered with him the Germans were no longer interested in offering resistance. Hands went up and Billy approached an older German who could have been the one who had just fired on them before they entered killing some of Billy's platoon behind him. All the other enemy close by had surrendered, hands above their heads speaking in their panic filled German language. Billy pointed his revolver at his face and fired the last round into his face killing him instantly. His comrades around him cried in shock, some wept in pain. At this point Eddie arrived pensively into the trench, behind too many of his men. He looked at the dead German. The reaction to Billy's murder of the German was mixed. Some of their company simply put eyes to the floor, others attempted to kill some Germans themselves, some succeeding before Sgt Robbins stopped them. The trench should be consolidated and the trench mortars found and neutralised. The noise had reduced and Billy ordered Robbins to take the advance along the trench.

They were finally in. They all knew they had just minutes to do their job, before reinforcements would arrive and kill them all.

'Komerad, Tommy Tommy, we no want to fight, our hands are up Tommy, don't shoot Tommy.'

Billy lunged forward, violently dragging the English speaking German towards him.

'Right, you speak English, fucking great. Now listen to me you bastard, you and four of your fucking friends are coming with us. You need to get back with us quickly you cunts I want you to run with us as fast as you fucking can. Do you hear me you cunt? As fast as you can. If any of you linger or try to get away I will shoot you right in the fucking face.'

Billy was screaming now in a wild voice, instilling fear on all those around him, German and English.

'Eddie, look after this prick while I look for a dugout and get some officers.'

'Let's just take these and fucking go Billy, their reinforcements will be here soon.' Eddie replied while Robbins returned telling them the whole line had their hands up.

Billy was reloading his pistol as the rain grew yet heavier and ignored Eddie's pleas.

The trench was now filled with more and more English, but Turner's Platoon had correctly stayed in their position in No Man's land to cover their return. Turner was a wise young lad. Billy took his platoon and stormed off along the trench in the other direction, while Eddie stood prostrate in the enemy trench. The soldiers defending the trench all had now given up and Eddie's Sergeant set up a line to ensure any German support met with a warm welcome. Billy ran around the traverse and found a dugout into which he and a dozen of his men rushed into, firing as they went. They met with no resistance and found more surrendering Germans, this time officers. Billy noticed one shoving papers on a fire, shot the offending officer in the back and took what remained of the burnt papers, burning his fingers in the process. The dug out was dark and dingy and full of smoke from the artillery shells which had successfully fallen close by. These officers had still been cowering in this dugout while their soldiers made a pitiful attempt to defend the trench.

Billy suddenly heard Eddie's voice as loud as it could have been. Then there was rifle fire, followed by machine gun fire. The German reinforcements were arriving.

Billy took two German officers and issued the same instruction that their English speaking comrade had received. They left the dugout and Billy gave the order to throw a bomb into it as they left to one of his men, who reluctantly obeyed.

Men's screams were followed by a dull explosion inside the dugout, followed by cries of pain. Billy by then had returned to Eddie's position with his prisoners and gave the order for them all to get out and get back as soon as they could. The flares had stopped allowing them to retreat in total darkness, but the moment they left the German trench, the reinforcements had nothing to hold them back. It was more difficult to leave this trench than it was to enter. There were no ladders on hand to use and a race developed between the returning Germans and the scrambling British. Another piece of poor planning. These were the details that could be the difference between life and death. It was a difficult evacuation especially with six prisoners to drag against their will. Men fell on the slippery muddy walls made worse by the heavy rain which now had drenched the area and men. Billy realised that this was a race they would soon lose so quickly gave up trying and searched the trench for a German machine gun with which to keep the enemy at bay. This was found and with the help of the same private who helped him earlier, the awkward maxim gun was placed in position while other men responded to Sgt Robbin's order to find some items to climb on. There were some thirty British in the German trench with half a dozen lying dead or dying above the trench. Some panic began to spread and Eddie was among those who were more concerned with worrying than finding a solution.

The maxim machine gun was set up in the direction of the traverse in the trench system aimed at the approaching Germans but it was these Germans who had already positioned their weapon and its deadly contents were suddenly released on the desperate invaders. In an instant the tiny area in which they were confined became a mass of flying lead and falling soldiers. While bodies gave protection from the fire, a heap of ammunition boxes were assembled giving some assistance to the men desperate to escape this flying death. From such close range the effect of the ten rounds per second was devastating. The falling bodies at least served to mask the gun that Billy was now trying to use and, although rounds were spitting all around him, some ricocheting off his own gun, he managed to answer the call of the Germans gun and quickly killed the entire crew manning it. This resulted in a momentary pause in the advance of the remaining Germans, allowing more time for Billy's men to escape. Leaving almost half their number dead or maimed, one by one they left. The prisoners were roughly pushed up against the trench wall and a young soldier discovered that a dagger in the arse helped them find the will and energy to climb the boxes and accompany their captors back to their lines with blood pouring from wounds caused by the daggers. There were only four captives now as two lay on the floor in the mud, perforated by the machine gun rounds of their friends. The scene was one of confusion and panic with men continuing to fall all around from rifle fire of German soldiers. Billy maintained his position on the machine gun along with the young brave soldier who he later learned was named Sloan. After a few seconds the pair had used all the rounds attached to the gun and there was certainly no time to reload the bloody thing. It had done its job well as without it there would have been no way of covering the retreat. Billy was impressed as Sloan picked up the gun and threw it over the trench so as not to allow the Germans to use it on them as they headed back to the safety of the British lines. Billy took some bombs from the dead and wounded British of which there was an increasing number, and threw them in the direction of the traverse. The British who had left had the same idea, ably instructed by a commander that Billy knew would not have been Eddie who had managed to escape and was probably running back for his life. This was almost as effective as the machine gun and the numerous explosions were met with more shrieks from wounded and dying men. Leaving over a dozen men on the floor of the blood filled and muddy trench the pair made an attempt for the boxes and miraculously scrambled out without being hit by the many rounds that smacked against the walls as they climbed. Finally out, Billy surveyed the situation. Young Turner had held his position and was now offering cover fire with his platoon from their shell holes in no man's land equidistant between the German and British front lines. The fourth platoon had completely disappeared and it could only be assumed that they were lost in the darkness of no man's land. The remaining two platoons were charging back with the prisoners having to be dragged each step. There was one hundred and fifty yards to safety and Billy and Sloan found a gap in the wire and began running with their backs to the enemy. It was difficult to remain upright, they both slipped and fell and crawled in the direction home with rain pouring down and rifle fire all around in the complete darkness that would mask their escape. But the darkness did not last. Within five minutes of leaving the trench, another series of flares climbed into the sky, exploding to expose the British positions in perfect clarity for the incensed Germans seeking retribution and revenge with only a dozen raiders in the open left to punish for their outrageous impertinence. It was then that a wave of rifle fire covered the pot marked field which separated them. In the light Billy saw Eddie; some thirty yards ahead of him fall in a manner not consistent with diving for cover. The remaining men fell to the ground, seeking the protection of a local shell hole. Turner's platoon answered this fire but attracted the attention of a machine gun that sprayed this position hitting two riflemen and making the others slip back into the water filled hole. Without the cover fire from Turner they were dangerously exposed in this position but Billy was determined to reach his friend in his time of need. Forgetting everything and everybody else he dashed and slid his way towards him. Within seconds he reached Eddie who was lying in a pool of mud, partially protected by the undulating ground. To their right was the group that had the prisoners, pinned down and as helpless as the rest. One of the Germans in this group was resisting and attempting to encourage escape when he was promptly shot through the head by a private, thus destroying any further dissention from his terrified comrades.

'Eddie!', he screamed, making himself heard above the din. 'Eddie.' He held him and noticed smoke from his tunic and looked down to see a black smoking hole below his chest.

Billy winced his eyes and looked to the sky and shouted 'No, No, No', as if such denial could change anything.

'Help me Billy, don't leave me Billy, get me back.' Eddie struggled to say then screamed as intense pain seared through his twisted and contorted body. At that time some soldiers entered the hole asking for orders. But there were none, they were all pinned down now, at the mercy of the Germans. The rifle and machine gun fire aimed at them continued and was joined by trench mortars that landed close by, blowing the mound away that offered cover for Billy, Eddie and the newly arrived men.

At the very time that despair seemed the only approach, salvation appeared as if from heaven. The officers back in the British trench had identified the true course of events and organised another artillery barrage. This was hastily prepared but very effective as the entire length of the German line now rose up in smoke and falling mud, taking those manning the firing line with them. This gave the British a chance to move and they all rose as one in a final dash to safety. The group with the prisoners reached the British line and Turner's platoon moved back in sections leaving an ever decreasing number in the shell hole providing covering fire. The last to leave was Turner himself who, facing the Germans and walking backwards, shot from his hip as he retreated back.

Billy did not move. He stayed with Eddie, keeping his hand pressed firmly to his wound as Eddie cried like a child.

'Don't go Billy.'

'I won't go, I'm with you till we both get back.' Billy could not bear the idea of losing Eddie, not now. He had to get him back to a clearing station where his wound would be tended and he'd be sent home. All they needed to do was get back. At that moment Billy heard his name called again. He looked back to find that Turner had walked backwards, straight into the British wire and was impaled in the middle of the sea of wood and wire, much as Billy had been almost two years ago. As Billy turned, the British artillery stopped and Billy knew it would not be long until the Germans returned and opened fire on a clear upright target that was Lt Turner.

'Stay right here Ed, I'll be back in one second.'

'No Bill, No, don't go.'

'I'll be straight back Eddie, I will not leave you. Look at me.' He shouted at the top of his voice and Eddie was quiet and looked at him. 'I will be straight back for you I will not leave you.'

At this Billy crawled the fifteen yards behind him to the wire where Turner stood. This was another thirty yards from safety. He tiptoed through and grabbed the young officer with both hands around the shoulders, giving him a huge, violent pull. Turner gasped in pain, the wire cutting into his skin, but still he was caught. Turner himself was carrying wire cutters which

Billy took and began the laborious process of cutting the wire, strand by strand. More time passed and they were all aware that soon the Germans would open fire. The three officers along with several badly wounded soldiers were now the last living British left out in no man's land and all were aware that time was running very low for them all. Many flares now occupied the night sky which helped Billy finally release Turner, just as the rifle fire from the Germans started again. Billy and Turner felt the bullets fly around their ears and Turner, now completely caked in wet mud headed back for the British Line. Turner was astonished to see Billy run in the opposite direction, out deeper into no man's land towards his stricken friend.

The rifle fire became intense and Billy was forced to dive for cover in the mud. Eddie was laying some ten yards from Billy but now very exposed as the lip of the shell hole he occupied was open. Billy, one hand on his tin helmet, looked over at his desperate friend who gazed upon him with desperate eyes. He held out a hand and called Billy's name, attracting the attention of the Germans who had perfect vision of the fallen British Officer. Billy could see that if Eddie were to move just a few feet to his right he would be behind another mound which would obscure the Germans and block their fire. He called as loud as he could for Eddie to move, but he was frozen and incapable of any movement. He gazed at Billy, now with pitiful almost resigned eyes as a round glanced off his helmet, not piercing it, just deflecting on its way. 'No' Billy screamed as another round splashed inches from Eddie's face splattering mud around.

'Eddie, Eddie.' Billy screamed again.

The German soldier had Eddie now in his sights. Two rounds had missed, this one wouldn't. He aimed, slowly squeezed his trigger and released the round. It flew the hundred yards that separated them and entered Eddie's jaw, blowing the left side of his face away. At this Eddie, inexplicably rose to his feet as a dozen rounds flew through the air hitting him all over his body. Billy rose himself, caring not whether death would follow. A round hit Eddie's lower arm, severing his hand above the wrist. Eddie raised his severed arm to his face and looked over at Billy, with complete desperation in his eyes. Billy now reached him, pushing him towards the ground as the German soldier who took his jaw, fired one more which hit Eddie centrally in the back of his head, exploding his skull and covering Billy with his minced and bloodied brains. Both men hit the floor and Billy held his friend who had nothing above the line of his upper lip. Mud, blood and gore covered Billy and he laid with his friend, now fully aware that he was dead, killed by concentrated rifle fire, much as one in a firing squad. Billy looked at his headless friend and called to the sky, hands aloft.

The surviving British very bravely climbed up out of their trench and fired at the German lines, beckoning the two back. Lt Turner, covered by this fire reached Billy again and pulled him back towards him. Billy was content to stay and die with his friend, but an urge to get Eddie's body back helped him get to his feet, carry Eddie's lifeless body and, with Turner's help, they reached the British Trench where they fell in a heap together over the parapet.

Billy laid his friend on the floor of the trench and covered it with his own great coat. He would not allow any one to touch Eddie until the medical orderlies arrived and Billy sat with his knees bent up looking through his legs at his mutilated friend's feet that emerged from his dirty muddy shroud. Still it rained, still Billy sat, slowly losing the will to live.

While he sat in the rain and mud the prisoners were led past him. The English speaker stopped and spoke to Billy.

'Why did you do that Tommy? Why? You killed my friends and we killed your friends for what? For nothing. Why did you do that Tommy? Why'

Billy looked up at him and although being led away, the German continued.

'No reason, no reason. Stupid Tommy, Stupid Tommy.' The German was crying as he shouted his words.

'You killed my old friend, shot him in the face, why Tommy?

Why? You did not need to do that. A stupid trench raid that will yield you nothing and now you cry for your dead friend who would be alive if you do not do this stupid raid. Stupid bastard Tommy. YOU are a cunt. You cunt!'

He continued his tirade as he was taken forcefully away.

You are so right my friend, so fucking right, he thought to himself. Billy put his face in his muddied hands and cried. He had failed to save his friend. He had ignored his friend during this raid. He had failed Eddie and his family. Billy broke into despair as the rain fell on his tired and withered body. He wondered in his mind how he would ever recover from this.

Twenty five dead British, with almost a dozen more badly wounded, some still in no man's land. Three Germans captured and plans seized by Billy. The trench raid was a success. The Divisional headquarters will be pleased. How nice. The prisoners surrendered some information that was of some value. The papers that Billy took were of some value. The raid was of some value to the British Army. It was of no value to Billy. He had lost his closest friend in horrific circumstances. The last few moments he had with Eddie will always be with him, for the rest of his days. The look of fear and panic in his friend's eyes. The devastating injuries he had sustained. It was just too awful to contemplate, yet contemplate this subject he did, time and time again.

He attended the field funeral that was hastily but reverently conducted by the Padre. The Major attended and said some words over Eddie and the eight other dead that they had managed to recover from No Man's land, although they all knew a further group laid dead or dying in the German trench or deeper parts of No man's land.

All the soldiers from the regiment dearly wanted to recover the bodies of these men, but the nature of the recent raid would ensure that they could expect no goodwill from the Germans they were facing and any attempt to venture above the parapet to recover the dead was met with accurate fire. They did have Lt Eddie Tompkin and he was buried along with men from his regiment, sharing a grave with them just a mile from where they fell. Billy was pleased that the body of Sloan was recovered and he lay next to Eddie. Billy stood frozen at the ceremony, still unable to accept Eddie's death. As he looked at his body, covered in a faded shroud, he pictured the condition of his face and how he looked the last time Billy saw him.

Chapter 17

The cap on the young lad was fixed slightly askew, his bicycle slightly too big for him but he cut an attractive figure as he rode through the countryside with his almost empty satchel and his book full of signatures. His was a rather depressing job of delivering telegrams, the vast majority of news from the front, the majority of these informing of tragedy. His vision had come to be more dreaded than that of the grim reaper.

On this bright spring morning he was looking forward to his final delivery and then back home for his lunch which his mother would now be preparing. This one was again from the War Office, this one small standard envelope bringing as much misery to a quiet quarter of Hertfordshire as a whole battery of artillery could to France.

He knew the house well as he took the final bend at speed and accelerated up to the driveway, crunching stones beneath his tyres almost mimicking the sound of thousands of tiny marching soldiers. As he entered the property he first saw Mrs Tompkin watering some baskets which hung above the door. Standing on a wooden chair she turned to see him as he stopped his bicycle and awkwardly climbed off.

The sight of him instilled an instant horror to the woman as she dreaded what he had to deliver. As a frightened child reacts to a menacing wasp that enters a room, she was immediately thrown into a wild panic. The watering can dropped onto the tiny stones beneath, as the shaking woman gave out a shrill which was heart wrenching even to the delivery boy to whom such reactions to his presence were commonplace.

'No, no, no ……' she wailed while beating a retreat to the comfort and safety of her home. Her cries broke the tranquillity of the late spring morning as a crow flew out of his perch on a nearby oak tree, squawking as if in sympathy with the desperate woman.

The terrified woman entered the darkness of the open door, repeating the desperate call of No, but nothing could change the content of the dreadful message. The boy was now left alone somewhat shaken, still listening to the cries from within the grand flower covered house. He was about to approach and knock on the open door when a man emerged, confused about the source of such hysterics. Upon seeing the boy he realised and almost stumbled as he began to comprehend the implications of his visit. A profound look of tempered grief appeared on his face, but with straightened back he approached the boy like a brave man walking to his execution.

The boy reached out with the telegram and handed it to the man, which he took in a confident manner. The boy then lifted the signature sheet, which he duly signed with a steady hand.

'Thank you Sir' said the boy plaintively as he turned to pick up his fallen bicycle.

Mr Tompkin stared above the boy holding the telegram as if he knew exactly the message contained therein. There was a good chance of course that their boy had just been wounded and was indeed on his way home away from the people who wish him harm. Back to his mothers arms that would take care of him and never allow him to be subject to such terrible dangers again.

But no. He knew. With the continuing cries of his wife in his ears he slowly opened the letter and with a deeply inhaled breath he lowered his eyes onto the words written on the stiff and perfectly creased government paper.

'It is with great sadness and regret that we inform you of the …'

His heart seemed to move to his throat, breathing became difficult and the world around him seemed to disappear down a long dark tunnel, with all that was left being a man and a piece of paper.

His head lowered, his eyes welled up and he could not prevent the awful first whine of a person about to cry. He put his thumb and first finger across his eyes as his legs became so awfully weak. He tried to picture his son but could not see his face. His son who he had always encouraged to be a man and do what was right. His son, who was without doubt the finest man on earth, whose very existence made his own life such a wonderful place to be. He just could not picture his face.

The cries from within the house became more intense with the realisation that there was no comforting look, telling her it was a big misunderstanding, everything is all right, it was merely a telegram from your sister in Shropshire. Nothing of that kind. She stood at the door, daring to peak out at the back of her husband whose head was bowed and slightly bouncing in a rhythmical way, yet still trying to remain dignified. This was all that was needed to reaffirm the worst fears of any mother. Her son was dead.

With increased intensity her cries brought her to her knees, cries which would break the heart strings of any man, as sure as pliers cut the wire which lay all around Europe.

The boy climbed onto his bicycle and peddled to the end of the drive. He was leaving a household in tatters, a household that was happy before he arrived. Perhaps he was indeed worse than the Grim Reaper. As he turned the corner at the bottom he felt compelled to stop and look back at the scene he had left. He noticed the figure of a hunched up boy leaning awkwardly on a walking stick surveying the scene before him of his two parents in torture. The cripple then caught the boy's eye, of all the scenes that had greeted him this morning, the look on the cripple's face was by far the worst.

With embarrassment he peddled again, the machine below taking him away from this scene of desperation. This war is not only being fought and suffered on the battlefields he thought.

His Mother had told him there might be cheese for lunch. That would be nice. He hadn't had cheese for a while. As he peddled along the country lane, he felt a quite warm sun on his face. The birds in the bushes sang as he rode past gathering more speed with every rotation of the pedals. Despite his upsetting morning he felt quite good. He even began to whistle.

Chapter 18

Although he had recently returned from leave, Billy was given three extra days to go with the decoration he would receive for his part in the raid. Billy was pleased to hear that Lieutenant Turner was also to receive a decoration along with Sgt Robbins and several others. Billy knew he had just one place to go, back to Hertfordshire, to Eddie's family who would have had the telegram delivered with the dreadful news.

When he reached their ivy covered house, he was greeted with a very warm yet solemn welcome. The family had organised a memorial service for their dear boy and Billy was impressed by the number of people attending. How different was the visit compared to the last one which was one of joviality, drunkenness and womanising. Mrs Walsh did attend but Billy could not bring himself to look at her. Whether she looked at him, he did not know and did not care. Billy gave a speech at the service where he spoke without preparation on how Eddie had made the war bearable for him, how he was so well liked, how his coolness under fire, his natural leadership and his bravery was an inspiration to everyone who served with him. Billy did not tell how he loved this man, although he wanted to. He wanted to explain how this man made him feel things he had never felt, how his company was all Billy needed, just being with him made everything bearable. How Eddie would always give advice, telling how he would always urge him on, take every chance he had, not to hold back in anything and how youth would not last. How Eddie was, a friend of his.

Billy was the only man in uniform at the service and it made him feel pathetic. It was necessary to show respect to the family and they would want him to look resplendent and smart, as if to show the world that their boy was a British Officer who died doing his duty. Billy wanted to rip away the clothes and revert to his civilian attire and he felt that this uniform represented the foolishness that had deprived this lovely family of their lovely boy. But everyone else liked to feel that Eddie had died with honour and Billy would perpetrate that line for their sake.

When the service had finished, Billy took the invitation to stay the night. A number of guests went to the house for a while but soon everyone had left and Mr and Mrs Tompkin retired to bed leaving Billy on his own in the cosy room by the fire. They discretely left him with a bottle of whisky for the evening which was gratefully received. Billy wanted to see Douglas, but he had not seen him since the service and he was nowhere to be seen at the house. From his appearance at the service Billy knew that he was suffering, but he wanted to see him, he wanted to talk with him, talk about Eddie. He sat back in the comfortable chair, opened the whisky and watched the flames as they performed their dance, like pagan virgins, around dried logs in the fireplace. On his mind was Eddie's face, his beautiful face. But Eddie was gone, now lying in a muddy patch of ground with his head blown away with worms and the creatures of the soil working diligently at the role they are on earth to perform. Billy's heart was breaking. If only he had stayed with him. If only they had left the German trench earlier. If only Eddie's platoon provided covering fire instead of Turner's. If only Billy had been killed instead, or as well.

His thoughts were broken by the sound of creaking floors and footsteps approaching. The wooden tap before each footstep told Billy of the arrival of Douglas at last. There was a fumbling of the door handle and after some time it opened to reveal the hunched figure of Eddie's brother. His eyes were bloodshot and his face pale. Douglas strained a painful smile at Billy and moved over to the chair closest to the fire and sat down, while Billy poured him a large one. For a moment neither spoke until Billy delivered the crystal glass, more than half filled with whisky.

'Thank you.' He took the glass, held it and asked Billy the question.

'You were there? There with him, when, it happened.'

'Yes I was Douglas, right with him, right at the end.' Billy replied.

With shaking hand Douglas took a large gulp and winced at the strength of the drink he was unused to. His gaze was held by the fire which was slowly dying through lack of attention.

'You'd have been very proud of him Douglas, he was so brave.' There was no reaction.

Billy spoke in a soft voice. 'You see mate, there were so many killed, always. It was almost impossible to get out of it alive. I am just a freak case I suppose. But what I'm saying is, he never really had a chance, none of us did. He knew it would happen and it did.'

Douglas answered in a whisper. 'Well no-one back here sees it that way, we all thought he'd come home.'

There was no answer to this and Billy did not offer one. They both sat for a while, lost in their own deep thoughts. The remarks seemed aimed at the fire as both sets of eyes were transfixed in that direction.

'He always made me feel like a real man, which, I suppose I'm not really. He gave me nothing but encouragement my whole life and included me in everything'.

He smirked and gazed at the quiet glow of the fire.

'How can I be anything without him, I am back to being a nothing and a cripple, sent before my time into this breathing world, scarce half made up.' He looked up, smiling at his very apt Shakespearian quote.

'I remember when war was declared we all went into town and cheered and danced around the clock tower. All young men, most of whom are dead now, and me. I knew that I would not be able to go but I cheered and showed enthusiasm just like the rest of them'. He held his hypnotic gaze at the fire place but his eyes began to well. 'That's how he made me feel'. He paused looked up at Billy and whispered again. 'That's how he made me feel.'

He turned, half fell on his stick and stumbled out of the room. Billy's eyes never left him as he watched him slowly walk up the hall to the foot of the stairs. As he began to climb he started to cry, his cries spreading through the cold, lonely house.

'Oh Eddie, O my dear Eddie, don't leave me alone.....' his pleas died out as his journey lengthened and was drowned completely with the closing of his door.

Of all the scenes Billy had witnessed through this war, this was one of the most painful. His vision was blurred through his tears as he collapsed on the chesterfield and muttered 'this fucking war, this fucking fucking war'. The fire continued to burn.

There he stayed until morning. He awkwardly said his goodbyes to the family after a breakfast which he hardly touched. Nobody seemed to talk much and he insisted on walking to the station rather than accept the ride that was offered. He held Douglas tight as he left and told him they would meet again soon and talk more about Eddie.

He swung his kit bag over his shoulder and began the three mile walk to the station. Time to contemplate more. The effects of yet another sleepless night tired his legs and behind him he left a sad and lonely household.

The train took him to London from where he would board a train to the coast on the following day, followed by a transport back to France. The railway station at Victoria was packed to the very rafters. Soldiers were everywhere, moving in every direction, some boarding trains some alighting, distinguished by the neatness of their uniforms. Some of these men were in the front line just hours previously and their boots carried the caramel coloured mud that clung to everything like so many leeches. Many wounded were being stretchered or carried along the busy platforms and Sergeants shouted at everyone, including the VAD nurses who accompanied the wounded men with sympathetic and exhausted eyes. The smoke from the trains covered huge swathes of people that appeared and disappeared with the intensity of the steam. There were also countless civilians, parents, children and sweethearts of returning and embarking soldiers, some crying some cheering and waving flags. Every tea hut was surrounded by bustling men in uniform as was every pub close by was full. It was through this chaotic atmosphere that Billy passed. As he left the station heading towards Buckingham Palace road, an attractive woman approached him, as working women would descend on Officers in the expectation that they not only held money but also felt paying was commonplace. There was no trade for this lady though. Billy walked through her as though he were a ghost. For a ghost was how he felt. He was facing a new sensation of gloom, one which had an intensity he had not experienced. He was to take lodging at an Officers' club in Pall Mall, between Trafalgar square and St James's. The brief walk from the station in the balmy evening air should have been pleasant. There were many people around, some in uniform, many, many not. It bothered Billy that people were carrying on their lives as though nothing was happening over there. But the human condition does that, people do carry on, despite adversities. As the tired expression has it, Life goes on!

He passed the Palace, walking down the Mall and turning left past Clarence House.

He was an impressive sight. His pristine uniform now contained two shining pips on each shoulder as he had been made full Lieutenant. His boots were shining, uniform clean and crisp and his Sam Browne strapping gave him the look of a distinguished British Officer. But this was a long way from the way he felt.

The Royal residence to his left had guardsmen in bearskins standing like statues on the road. A Sergeant was in the process of examining them when he noticed Billy walk by. Noticing Billy's uniform, he stood to attention, stiffly saluted and said 'Evening Sir.'

A young boy with his mother walking by witnessed this greeting and stopped while holding his mother's hand. 'Look Mummy' he said drawing her attention to the salute. The boy was impressed and his mother looked Billy in the eyes and gave him a smile, a smile Billy recognised. Billy was already a hero to the boy and a potential plaything for his mother. Both reactions disgusted him. He had just had enough. Billy hurried past the two, not offering any response to either.

He began to feel tired and his head began to spin as he walked along as giddy as a drunken man. Unable to focus, he needed shelter, needed to find his residence before he broke down. He approached the Officer's club with two large lanterns hanging from the wall. A corporal checked his papers, eyed his medals and cheerfully let him pass with another stiff salute. Billy took his key and headed up the stairs wanting nothing but his bed. The closer he got to his room, the faster he went, desperate for the refuge of his private room. He opened his door, threw his kitbag down and fell face first on the bed, sobbing like a child. He felt eternally lonely. He felt that his sunken heart could never be salvaged; this deep gloom could only be his permanent state of mind forever. He drenched the stiff white pillow with his tears, the saltiness mixing with the coarseness of the pillow case to sting his face. Finally he fell into a deep, haunted sleep. He was walking into a dugout which was also a classroom from his old school. As he entered, Eddie turned around to look at him.

'Lieutenant Mercer! Great to meet you. Eddie Tompkin.'
Billy woke with a startled jump. His face was contorted by the awkwardness of his position on his damp pillow. He sat at the side of the bed holding his head in his hands. Outside the sun had left the sky, replaced by darkness, suggesting Billy had slept for some hours. After a long bath Billy dressed again and ventured downstairs to find some food. He met the same corporal who arranged for sausages and eggs to be cooked, despite the lateness of the hour. Billy was alone in the large reading room that overlooked Pall Mall. There was still activity outside with drunken soldiers singing into the night as they returned to barracks nearby. Billy was brought a bottle of wine which made him smile as he looked at the label. Chateau Margeaux. Hmm. This bottle was despatched within

ten minutes, to be swiftly replaced with a new one. When this was finished, Billy decided to take the night air. He walked up St James's onto Piccadilly. He passed the pubs and hotels and was confronted by a vibrant atmosphere which confused him. He wondered where the money that was being spent was coming from. Civilians were out as well as military men, prostitutes in almost every doorway and by the time he reached Piccadilly Circus he had received some extraordinary offers in return for payment.

He walked aimlessly down the Haymarket, through the square and onto Whitehall. He caught his reflection in a window as he passed by. The sight stunned him and he froze to examine himself. He could not recognise himself. He had lost weight on his face, he appeared thin and gaunt and was deathly pale. He stared at his reflection, not liking what he saw. Hating what he saw. Hating himself. Why was he still alive when all he had loved was dead? He had nobody, nobody to talk to, nobody to remind him that the human race were not solitary beings but social animals. He had no mind to talk to anybody on a personal level, as everything he has ever cared for was gone. He walked; shoulders slouched, past the Houses of Parliament onto Westminster Bridge. Only one person could save him. Only Eddie. He needed Eddie.

He leaned over the wall of the bridge as a car raced passed with headlights lighting the scene. He looked over to St Paul's and noticed a flicker of the dawn emerging from that direction. The street lamps will be extinguished soon, he thought as he looked down onto the flowing water at high tide. How powerful the river seemed. Flowing indefatigably under him, the river he had played in as a child, the river that made London what it was, and London made Billy what he was. He was a function of this river. It could take him away from his desperation. Take him home. Its inky blackness could save him. He stood on his toes, raising himself, looking down into oblivion.

Old Father Thames kept rolling along, but without him. As the sun rose over the river it brought with it thoughts of a new life. The darkness limped away; disappointed it had failed in the contest for Billy's soul. The light had saved him. He went back down Pall Mall and slept the best sleep for many years.

The next afternoon he was on a train to Dover.

Chapter 19

The journey back to the front seemed to take forever. There were delays on the trains to Dover, delays on the transports to Calais and no trains at all to take him back to the front from there. All the inconveniences were lost on Billy as he completed the entire journey with his head down and thoughts elsewhere. It was not so long ago that he took an identical route with Eddie when returning from their leave at his parents' place. That time they had laughed and talked the entire way. Stopping at Dover for a liquid lunch, continuing their refreshment on board the transport across the channel and even more drinking as they waited in Calais along with a 'quick one' in a brothel that came highly recommended by a Lieutenant from D company. He made the same footsteps this time, but with shoulders more hunched and a back less straight. He had the air of one who should be left alone. His drink now came from a flask which was regularly topped up from a fine bottle of Scotch provided by Mrs Tompkin, which was thrown overboard when empty. He watched it bob away in the sea, seemingly back to England while he headed to France.

Finally, some forty eight hours after leaving Hertfordshire, he arrived at reserve lines where he would rejoin the regiment. He was greeted with the news that he would be promoted to captain as the losses were quite appalling from the last show and officers were very few. He was told that this was some kind of record for the British army, for a man to rise from private soldier to Captain in two years. He was told he would be recommended for some new medal to go along with this Military Medal and this was most likely the reason for his promotion. The Brigadier General would be presenting it the following day at Brigade headquarters where Billy was told to attend. After a long night's sleep, he dressed as smartly as he could and made his way over.

Brigade HeadQuarters were four miles from the front. The

location was fairly precarious as a break through by the Germans in this sector would result in the potential loss of some senior Officers if they could not be evacuated in time. Not as grand as divisional HQ which were usually French Chateaux, this was more like a Manor House, but well appointed with enough room for Brigadier General Wilton and his staff of fifteen along with the fifty or so other staff who were housed in the grounds or nearby village.

Billy was instructed to wait in a very fine hallway before finally being summoned to see the General. He walked in proudly and saluted smartly and correctly.

'Welcome Lieutenant' he said, returning his salute, 'Come on sit down, make yourself comfortable. Can I get you a drink?'

'Whisky would be very nice Sir' Billy replied with a slight confidence as he immediately felt himself an equal to this man.

'Fine, fine.' He paused slightly as he looked at Billy. 'Scarlett!' he called out to his servant who was fussing around close by, 'Pour myself and Lieutenant Mercer a nice large glass of my special reserve would you'

They were both sitting in fine armchairs as the drink arrived and Wilton again looked at Billy and asked him to retell his glorious trench raid for which he would receive a decoration and then his entire war experience and his opinions and thoughts on the progress of the war. Billy gladly and openly told his account, without modesty, as the next few hours passed and the General's special reserve drained away.

The General was a slim man of some fifty years old. He was known as quite a character around the general staff and was very popular due to his gregarious outlook and his aristocratic heritage. He felt himself to be a humanist however and was a strong advocate of soldiers from the ranks becoming officers. He had heard about Mercer before, when he was commissioned and took a particular interest in his progress. This meeting had filled him with some form of trepidation as he came face to face with a man who had seen the real face of this war and yet was now in the required officer class which would allow him to converse with a General over a glass of fine Scotch.

Brigadier General Wilton had seen fighting in the Boar war where his company opened fire on a troop of despatch riders who had come too close to a British Column. A man from his platoon had hit the bearded Dutchman and they all stood around his lifeless corpse as photos were taken. That was the only time he had seen fighting first hand as the current conflict had only seen him many miles behind the lines. He had regretted that fact and often wished to visit a front line trench but this was vehemently forbidden. Even a Colonel was never encouraged to venture such risks and Brigadier General Wilton was Brigadier General Wilton before the war and had seen no promotional advancement to mirror that of his present companion.

His grandfather had fought with the Scots Greys at Waterloo, his father with the Hussars with the Heavy Brigade in the Crimea, and so he was always destined to be a cavalryman. His commission swiftly followed his final year at Eton and the proud Subaltern had risen to Brigadier over the next thirty years but never to beyond like his forebears. Still time I suppose. Perhaps a gallant brigade assault would be enough. That, along with his being a Baron would suffice surely. He had given the Army his life and had gone for a long period as a Bachelor, until he had met the daughter of a subordinate officer who was keen to see her married. It made perfect sense to all that he be married and young Melissa was a beautiful and perfect choice. All except his bride, who dutifully went along with the marriage so as not to upset her dying Father. Melissa never imagined marrying a man some twenty eight years her senior but the entire family had made it so difficult for her.

'The Baron is so very rich, we shall all be so well looked after. Baroness Wilton, how lovely hehehe!' Hmm.

A lucky man in this respect was Wilton. Melissa was so beautiful although her beauty seemed lost on him. Still, General Robertson attended the wedding as was the Duke supposed to, but he was detained elsewhere. And a fine wedding it was, so very fine.

Wilton was stunned by the story of Billy Mercer. He was fascinated by the experiences that this young man had. This man knew more of the war than anybody he has met and immediately wanted him on his staff, wanted him advising him, wanted him as part of his team. He recognised this would involve promoting Billy to Captain, which was awkward as the young man had probably been promoted too much already, but Wilton was a Brigadier General and he can do what he feels is best.

Having Mercer around him would be best. Best for his regiment, best for his brigade, best for…

Mercer's eyes were fixed on the roaring log fire as his mind recalled Eddie's face again. His eyes were open, but he was not reading the picture they presented. He was thinking of and missing his friend and the image of his decimated body lying in his arms came back. Again.

'You have had a good war Lieutenant'.

Mercer's eyes slowly moved from the flickering flames to the eyes of Wilton. Modestly raised eyebrows were his only response to Wilton's conclusion to his story.

'And as such you have earned the MC. Usually there would be a far grander ceremony but in these times I will hand it to you myself. Along with that I would like to offer you a place on my staff as an Adjutant. I know that you will be a huge asset to our planning team and I would like to welcome you aboard. You will be promoted to Captain and will start the position as soon as you can settle things with your platoon. There is a new subaltern arriving who I would like you to meet and show the ropes to. Just a youngster you know. I suppose that is rather a lot for you to take in Captain, but congratulations to you my dear boy.'

He stood up and Mercer followed. He shook hands firmly with the young Captain and held his gaze. Wilton was smiling at him broadly, with his eyes as well as his mouth, making

Mercer slightly uncomfortable as he held his hand slightly too long. But Billy was pleased. This role would get him away from the mud and cold and death. Some would feel guilty to those left behind, but not him, not now. No way. He had seen enough and done enough in this war. Sit back and see out the war in cosy rooms like these and smoke cigars and drink fine Whisky and be involved in orders which he had objected to so many times when on the receiving end.

'I look forward to starting work as soon as possible General, and thank you so very much for this opportunity.'
Wilton finally released his hand and let him go.

'You will receive a new uniform, with three pips on your shoulder' he grinned after such an inane comment. All knew how many pips a captain has. 'I will let Colonel Price take you through your duties and I am sure you will get on famously. Ask for him as you leave as there are some papers for you to sign.'
Mercer stiffly saluted, turned in military style (feeling like a fool) and began to exit the room.

'You'll be able to wear your medals to work aye Mercer?' Billy turned to witness that smile again.

'Yes sir, that will be splendid' Mercer could take his whisky better than the General.

Mercer approached a reception style table and asked for Price. After ten minutes Price appeared and picked up some papers that were on the table. It was apparent to Mercer that this man was not reading them, rather pretending to do so.

'Colonel Price?'
No response as he continued his intense study of the papers.

'Colonel Price?'
Still he read.

'Oh, Major Price?' This solicited a response as Price turned to him. 'Colonel Price Mercer'

'Sorry Colonel. I was asked to report to you.'

'You were told to report to me and you will do so when convenient to me Mercer, not yourself. Now go upstairs to room 22 and wait until I return.'

'Yes Sir' Mercer replied in a voice that was far too loud.

Price was unhappy about the promotion of enlisted men, especially one as young as Mercer. He was determined to make his life as hard as possible, but had not accounted for one such as him.

It was not a good start of the relationship between these two and from these poor beginnings the relationship only deteriorated.

But Mercer was now in. In a special club of far easier living.

Chapter 20

Life in the general staff was even better than he expected. He was given an assistant, with whom he mainly only exchanged dirty jokes, a nice workplace, three hot meals per day and as much alcohol as he could consume. There were no lice in his uniform, no mud all over his uniform and no blood and other unmentionable matter on his uniform while working at the staff. The contrast was really rather profound. He found he had spare time on his hands which he spent in the library, supposedly studying military matters, but actually picking up the works of Shakespeare which he finally seemed to understand. His mother would always go on about the bard, with a quote for every occasion; it seemed her son was starting to concur. After just a month he became very popular with the more junior members of the staff and as the weather got warmer they would often play football on the finely kept lawns. He was working on a radio operator and making slow progress with her. Her face was not great but Corporal Judith Stone had a gorgeous figure and Mercer could barely take his eyes off her as she walked passed. Her blonde hair was rather short and a bit too military, but this woman had a genuine sexiness about her, a sexiness that she was unaware of. The young corporal had two brothers in the infantry and liked to ask Mercer questions about trench life and he tried to comfort her with lies. When she took the liberty of clutching his hand when he delivered good news about her brother's regimental movements, Mercer knew she was ready. Any time he wanted.

On a particularly hot evening, the staff organised a football match against another from their neighbouring headquarters. It was a very good idea and all the staff enjoyed making arrangements and discussing the make up of the team. Mercer and another Captain were the highest ranks on the 4th brigade staff team, although the 2nd had a full Colonel playing down the left midfield, in a holding position in behind the two strikers. He was rather a good player too.

Nobody thought about shirt colours so 4th Brigade played with shirts off. This was the first time that Billy's body was exposed and the scarring to his shoulders, back and neck drew the eyes of the other players and spectators. An acute triangle scar led from below his ear to the outside of his shoulder and the legacy of numerous lacerations upon his back was still visible. Remnants from his time on the wire. Where he lost his friends. His first friends.

Still, his muscular frame cut a nice figure and Judith could not suppress a small gasp when seeing his body for the first time. He had a small waist and broad shoulders and the curves on his body were as effective as those on a woman.

Many spectators watched this more than the game and Brigadier General Wilton was especially impressed with his new recruit's physical appearance. When the final whistle blew and his team had lost 4 goals to 1, Wilton dashed over to Mercer to congratulate him on, well, his loss.

'Well played Mercer, great game, great game. His arm went round his shoulder.

He looked at his scars from close range, almost asking a question.

'On the Somme Sir' answered him.

'O yes. Yes of course'

'Mercer, I was going to ask you. Right. Would you like to attend the Divisional Ball at Calais next month? It will be a stuffy affair but Earl Haig will be there and I would like to introduce you to some of the top brass. My wife will be there too, she is dying to meet you. Wants to meet a real hero what! Why don't you come aye? Why not?'

'Thank you sir, thank you.'

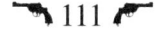

Chapter 21

It was the first opportunity for Billy to wear his entire staff uniform complete with his Military Cross and his Military Medal. A fleet of vehicles were leaving Brigade HQ carrying many invitees but Billy was by far the youngest and most junior in terms of rank. His inclusion puzzled some who took the journey but his decorations were the most impressive as his medals represented genuine bravery and were not as those awarded to the top brass for nothing much in particular.

While travelling with Wilton in the car, Billy started to imagine what the General's wife would be like. He pictured a dull old aristocratic type and he dreaded meeting her and answering banal questions. He allowed his mind to wander to Cpl Stone. She really was very pretty, he thought and he pondered on how he would be moving in for the kill when he had this inconvenient Ball out of the way.

After a two hour car ride, hearing from the general about who would be there with the necessary gossip attached, they arrived at the beautiful chateau that was playing host to the grand affair in Calais. A team of servants greeted every approaching car and the driveway was a host of the finest cars in Europe with elegant ladies, resplendent gentleman, military men, aristocrats and press people taking photos of everyone and everything with the flash bulbs puncturing the night like so many bursting artillery shells which were fortunately a safe distance away. Billy alighted from the car and was handed a drink along with everyone else, as if the short walk from the car to the Ballroom would have been unendurable without a drink.

It was another balmy summer's evening and although this was a very impressive affair with very impressive looking people, Billy was struck with how perverse this really was. Men were dying less than a hundred miles away while this lot were playing jolly hockey sticks, pissing it up and no doubt talking nonsense for the evening.

This was going to be bloody awful.

Wilton informed them that he would wait for his wife, Melissa, while the rest should join the crowds inside. Billy duly obliged feeling the need of a proper drink that he would find in the chateau. He entered the elaborate doorway with Price who immediately adopted the air of one who was used to such plush surroundings, while Billy clearly was not. The hallway was a kind of antechamber and they walked down its length accompanied by many ladies, some of whom were extremely attractive. But Billy's thoughts were on a good drink. The war had given him an undesirable dependence on strong liquor, but it appeared a small price when compared to what this war had done to so many others.

They reached the end where a footman stood taking the invitations from the queuing guests for they were all to be announced. Oh bloody hell, thought Billy, just about all I need! The footman took the card and whispered its details to a Sergeant Major type who bellowed them out to the other uninterested guests.

'Colonel Price' was shouted to the room without reaction. But the Sergeant Major type did his office fairly, for when he was handed Billy's card, which merely gave his name and rank, he met it with a swift glance, swift enough to notice his chest.

'Captain Mercer, MC, MM'

This created something of a murmur which died as it was born yet lived long enough to annoy Price.

What was of interest here was not so much the company of an MC, which was relatively rare, but the fact that he held also the Military Medal which meant he was originally an enlisted man who had risen through the ranks to become a Captain.

Billy offered his arm to Colonel Price, suggesting they walk in as a couple and offering an equally suggestive smile. Price was unamused by Billy's joke and rapidly put as much distance as he could between himself and the young impertinent Captain, spouting out some insult as he disappeared into the crowd.

The surroundings staggered Billy. It was the most impressive room he had ever entered and the sight of so many fabulously dressed people was something to behold. There were hundreds of people at this event, but this room contained them all in a comfortable manner. All around the walls were furniture of the very highest hand crafted quality, every inch of fabric on curtains and attached valances was silken and shining and new. The room had large French doors, well it was a Chateau after all. These doors were open allowing in a pleasant breeze and fine people stood around, taking drinks off robotic and perfectly attired serving staff and Billy was truly in wonderment at these surroundings. At that moment, almost in an effort to impress Billy yet more, the Orchestra suddenly burst into life and was greeted with a genteel round of applause. The powerful sound of Tchaikovsky's Sleeping beauty raised Billy's spirits and for the first time, Billy felt pleased that he had come. He reached over to a tray of champagne, winked at its server and took two glasses, downed one, placed it back on the tray and took another.

'I don't know when I'll see you again,' he said to the server, making an impression of a heartbroken lover.

The server, decades older than Billy managed the merest hint of a disapproving glance and walked quickly away, leaving a smirking Billy.

He looked around the guests to find that he was surrounded by the very highest of England's social set with probably every aristocratic family and every Regiment of the British Army represented. There were many senior and staff officers with far fewer combat officers present. O how he wished Eddie was here. He'd be fine if Eddie was around to joke with and cut a sway through this lot. That boy could pull a crowd for sure. Upon further inspection of the crowd, Billy was delighted to see the face of young Mr Turner standing with a group of other junior officers, feeling awkward amongst these surroundings. When he caught Billy's gaze his face lit up like a flare and within moments he was over, with his companions shaking Billy enthusiastically by the hand and telling all that were happy to listen about Billy Mercer, the bravest Officer in the regiment. Billy was very fond of this young man and he was genuinely happy to see him.

'What's a mere soldier like you doing here Turner? We don't like your type at our functions, you actually are involved with the war and that won't do at all. These events are reserved for those who don't have a clue about the front. I'll be writing a strongly worded letter to the War office social committee.' The accent Billy used ensured there was no seriousness in his remark.

Turner enjoyed the veiled compliment and smiled in a happy way to his friends. A compliment it was, but he was here at the invitation of his Father, a General who was across the room, looking at his son with proud eyes.

'Champagne Mercer? No whisky?'
Turner knew Billy well.

'Funny you say that, I was about to ask. I could do with a real drink'

'Look no further' excitedly exclaimed Turner as he delved into his tunic's inside pocket to release a silver flask. While he poured the contents into Billy's champagne glass, Mercer noticed how small and boy like were his hands. This poor lad had not even finished growing, yet here he was in fine dress uniform at the most fashionable military Ball in the country. He was so young but this war was being fought by the young and the elder soldiers were wasting their time at events like this. For a moment a hint of guilt entered his mind at this thought, while he pulled his gaze from Turners hands.

Turner poured himself one and momentarily neglected his friends.

'To Eddie,' he said. It hit Billy like a steam train. He looked up and whispered 'To Eddie' and they both drank the contents. The two men shared a moment that none who had not endured such experiences together ever could and envious eyes of Turner's friends could only guess at the true meaning of the toast. 'Thanks mate.'

Billy turned away to look at the other guests in more detail. There were some fabulous looking women at the event and Billy was looking forward to the proceedings as he was determined to forget his woes with the help of a willing lady and there were surely willing ladies here. A group of three young and shy girls walked by Billy, Turner and the three others and held their eyes for as long as they could until their resilience gave way to giggling. Billy smiled at them all and with a gesture to Turner, began the game they would all have liked to play tonight. The young officers laughed also, as did Brigadier General Turner who from afar was pleased to see that the purpose of inviting his son to this Ball was not forlorn.

Billy held out his glass towards Turner. 'Any reinforcements?'
Turner duly obeyed and started to fill the glass. Billy took his eyes from the pouring and looked up, straight at one of the most beautiful girls he had ever seen.

This girl was alone, looking around as if seeking somebody, but in a cursory manner which suggested an indifference to whether or not the person was located.

From several yards away Billy could notice the striking nature of her eyes, yet it was not so much the colour as the brightness. Much like a pebble that is the dullest of colours comes to life when correctly polished, her eyes sparkled seemingly around the room. Their hue was a light green and they gave the impression they were illuminated from behind as light projects on a slide to produce a bright and clear image. These were unique and Billy was drawn to them. Her auburn hair was in old fashioned ringlets which bounced off her cheeks and covered her ears and fell suspended over her shoulders. Even her hair had brightness and although her frame was rather petite, there was an air of complete healthiness about this girl and Billy was sure he had never seen anyone like her in his life. Although alone there was confidence around her and as her eyes darted around the room, they came to rest straight into the eyes of Billy Mercer. They both looked at one another almost as if they recognised each other. He couldn't take his eyes from her, he couldn't raise a smile as he dearly wanted. Something had a hold on him and his actions were no longer his own. It was she who finally allowed a smile and before he could respond he was blocked by the figure of General Wilton who approached her and kissed her cheek. Billy was truly interested in this encounter as he now had a good chance to meet this woman who clearly knew the General. He moved closer to discover that the General appeared angry with her.

'I told you to wait for me outside, how do you think this looks, me being announced alone? You really have no idea at all!'

The young woman was penitent and apologised in an awkward but heartfelt way.

Billy was shocked as he continued his approach. It could not be, he thought.

What a sly old dog the Brigadier is! How on earth has he married such a beautiful creature as this? Momentarily his regard for Wilton soured as there must be something rather special about the Brigadier if he had captured the heart of this woman. He was eager to engage with the couple and presented himself to his superior Officer.

'Ah Mercer, splendid! There you are. Well, let me introduce you to my wife' There was much pride in his eyes as he turned and beckoned his wife towards them, his wife's eyes already being firmly fixed on the young Captain.

'My dear, meet Captain Mercer, the hero of the 9th Battalion. Quite a laddie this boy is, seen it all haven't you Mercer?'

Wilton was proud of Mercer and proud of the appearance of his wife as he correctly believed that his standing in Mercer's eyes will be much augmented by the existence of such a stunning wife.

'Mercer, this is my wife, Melissa.'

Melissa held out her gloved left hand and Mercer bowed to kiss it.

'Good evening Lady Wilton' he said as he looked up at her.

'Good evening Captain' she replied, holding his gaze.

Something deep inside Billy seemed to move as he made contact with Melissa. He had known many women but none whatever had hit him as this one. He felt unable to talk and he inwardly cursed the reflex in a human that compelled one to act like a complete fool at the very time that you wanted it least. The Orchestra started up Blue Danube by Strauss and this sound broke Billy's trance. He did like this piece. Melissa and Wilton also turned and this Waltz was evidently a popular choice.

'Blue Danube,' exclaimed Wilton, 'your favourite. Melissa was dancing to this piece when I first saw her.' This remotely romantic remark was devalued by the way Wilton immediately turned away to greet Price along with several other Officers who appeared.

Wilton seemed in very good spirits and was remarkably affable to all those gathered around him.

Billy looked back at Melissa who reciprocated and, though their silence was not broke, their eyes a sweeter language spoke!

'Captain Mercer's mother was a dancer my dear, isn't that right Mercer?' Billy was intrigued as to how Wilton knew this but was impressed and grateful to him for bringing up such a subject as it seemed to interest Melissa.

'How exciting, I'd have loved to have been a dancer. Was your Mother on the stage?'

It seemed the conversation was a sideshow.

'In a few west end….' He did not have time to finish before Wilton interrupted, his remarks being far more important than everybody else's.

'And Mercer dances also I understand, the lion of the 9th has magic in his feet as well.'

It was beginning to be somewhat awkward and Wilton had finished flattering Billy, in an abject way and turned his ear to the conversation of the other Officers who gladly welcomed him in. Billy was uncomfortable and reacted as he always had, with decisive action.

'General, would you mind if I had the honour?'

Price was the first to react with a disapproving glance but the General was perfectly happy with the request but appreciated the slight impertinence. It somehow suited him to see his beautiful wife dancing with such a fine looking man. A strange sentiment but nevertheless genuine.

Billy took Melissa, who was somewhat shocked by the pace of it all, in his arms and she rapidly adopted the correct posture of a straight back with her arms around his back.

'I hope you don't mind Melissa' said Billy, more impertinence.

Melissa did not answer but merely stepped back as the first paces of their Waltz began. Billy deliberately led her away from their assembled entourage and then had the chance to look at her lovely face from such close distance. Melissa returned his gaze, thoroughly intrigued by this man. He was six inches taller than her despite her high shoes and Melissa could feel his strength through their embrace. They span around, adding the Viennese aspect to the Waltz and could see the faces of all were on them, most notably Price and the General. It began to become apparent that these two were very capable dancers and the quality of their movements made them stand out significantly from the vapid, tired dancing that shared the floor. Billy held her yet tighter and Melissa did not resist, allowing herself to be pulled in closer to him. Still they did not speak but their eyes remained locked on one another.

The General, with a loud and hearty 'Bravo', clapped his hands and took the chance to then turn away and continue his conversations. It was good timing for him for at that very time General Rawlinson approached him.

'General, how delightful to see you.'

'Wilton. Splendid'. The men shook hands as Price stood obsequiously by.

'My word Wilton, your wife can certainly dance. Who is the partner, have you hired him for tonight?' This weak remark was met with a guffaw of unjustified laughter and Wilton gladly told the General that the man in question was the highly decorated man that he was, appearing more proud of Billy than his wife. After a few more moments spectating, the men resumed into conversation, the proceedings on the dance floor being no longer of interest. All of them that is, except Price who was uncomfortable with the dance, but the two had now gone from sight, hidden and obscured by the numerous, less accomplished dancers.

Billy and Melissa were enjoying this dance. Their bodies moved very well together and their eyes never left one another. Melissa realised that she was very attracted to this man and the physical impact that he had on her was becoming difficult to disguise. His left arm that was around her waist contracted yet more, drawing her yet closer. Her reaction was again one of compliance and closer and closer they came until his thigh was positioned between her legs as they danced and became more pressed against her groin. This was particularly incongruous but to Billy's joy he felt her push this holiest part of her body onto him more as they spun around, oblivious to the world. If one had've had the inclination to closely examine them, their unbefitting moves would have been apparent, but nobody did notice, it was discreet and between them only.

Melissa had never had an encounter such as this. This one dance opened up a whole new life, a whole new perspective on what joy can be contained in the briefest of moments or experiences. The room began to spin for her and she felt suddenly very hot. Her face began to blush and Billy took this as his cue to retract, only for Melissa to thrust again forward as they spun again. At this point Billy looked into her fabulous green eyes and smiled. Melissa smiled back. The music stopped.

All stood around clapping, some older officers directed their applause at Billy and Melissa and within a flash they were joined by their previous company, Melissa whisked away to another part of the room. Billy stood frozen on the spot. Something had just happened, something wonderful. He walked in the other direction, in need of a drink. People parted as he walked by, his dancing and his appearance had made quite an impact on the other revellers.

The well crafted chairs lined the dance floor like a finely embroidered border. With her drink in her hand Mellissa found a vacant one and hurried to sit as though her legs could carry her no longer. From across the ballroom the ever present gaze of old faithful Michele, her maid, was on her watching her every move, living vicariously through this stunning young woman. Melissa gave her a generous smile, enough in the gesture to let her in completely on the state of her mind. The music played on so loudly as she looked around the room. Full of staff officers acting mostly like school boys. She began to feel a slight contempt for these gentlemen, none of them seemed to appear quite as smart as she used to think. As she watched she noticed how unathletic were a lot of their frames, small hunched shoulders, silly little sparrow legs. Not like his body. The strong body which was in her arms just moments before. Firm shoulders, rock hard arms. What would it feel like to have such arms around you when captured by sleep? Full breaths on her neck from strong healthy lungs, making the fine hairs dance.

She snapped out of it. My goodness, what thoughts for a respectable woman to have. She should be ashamed, she thought. To her alarm she felt a rush of moisture between her legs. She blushed as if the whole room knew and moved her thighs. She had never felt anything like this in her life even with physical assistance. This was a truly sexual experience. Although still somewhat affronted by Billy's impudence, at this moment she wanted only to see his face. She in fact wanted to dance with him again, never having danced in such a way before with so accomplished a partner. The orchestra played on approaching the crescendo of Pashobel's Canon, the music heating up along with her emotions. She strained her head, this way and that in an attempt to see him. Where was he, what was he doing, who was he with? His absence seemed to pain her, she felt compelled just to set eyes on him again, those shoulders, that waist. Still she peered unsuccessfully covering every corner of the ball room. Perhaps he had left, even been ejected by her fool of a husband. She caught her husband's eye as he disdainfully turned away. He could not have ejected him, he would be boasting to his imbecilic friends if he had. Still she searched like a lost lamb. Another old General walked in front of her view, but from between his arm and body she glimpsed a taller, younger figure. As the old man passed…there. It was him looking straight into her eyes. The crescendo of the music screeched out as if to capture the intensity of this moment. Foolishly she turned away, only to recapture his gaze just moments after. This time her inhibitions were weakening. Her stoicism wavering and as he recognised it he allowed himself to smile, smile like he wanted to smile, almost ear to ear. His eyes widened, his heart fluttered as he looked into the eyes of the most beautiful thing he had ever seen. She seemed so small and helpless yet at the same time radiating an air not of confidence, but self assuredness. The music blasted as he detected the first change of expression on her face. As she looked she responded to his smile, by smiling back but with her eyes. They seemed to gloss over and her mouth gave the most subtle of smiles. This expression was from her eyes, her eyes told him all he needed to know. The look then transcended into a full blown smile as her head lowered in a vain attempt to hide what her soul was dictating. Keeping her eyes upon him she could feel Michele next to her, witnessing the whole spectacle. She could not stop, no more did she want to, she wanted to take in all she could of the spectacle in front of her. Never had she been so physically attracted, nor emotionally intrigued about another human being. From that moment she wanted to know everything about him, she needed him with her, regardless of anything. He was supremely confident for a man so clearly out of his depth in terms of rank and social class. As her head lowered more she broke the gaze. He stood, in the middle of the floor, like a rabbit in headlights.

Billy had never known this feeling. He had never appreciated the softness and tenderness of a woman. But he knew, at this point, that the woman, who sat in front of him, must be his. He wandered around the room, almost in a daze, contributing to scattered conversations regarding the effectiveness of Artillery or Cavalry, when it struck him again how totally hopeless this situation was. Here he was, surrounded by the decision makers in this war, listening to discussions about Cavalry. In the lines he had seen, most horses would have sunk in the mud before they gained ten yards, yet still, these arseholes were debating the merits of this outdated and highly inflated fighting force. The red braids of the staff officers gave them a comical appearance, such comedy which was matched and occasionally even outdone by their hilarious words concerning the conduct of the war. In a way, he would rather be back in the trenches than surrounded by these people, eating canapés and drinking fine Gin and tonics. But on reflection, this was slightly more tolerable. What would his old friends make of this, make of his curious surroundings? But it did not matter, for now he had no friends, just acquaintances who he would like to see out the war with, go home, collect and sell his wine stash and live off the proceeds for a good long while. These were his plans in life, until he saw her. Now she must be involved. He looked around to catch another look at her to find she had vacated her seat. Opposite her chair was an open French door from which the breeze blew the delicate curtains into the form of contorted ghost like figure. He approached the door to see her figure standing at the balustrade overlooking the grounds. The sparkling sequins on her dress seemed to catch the sparse light and the breeze blew her gown around her body showing her firm figure and perfect form. It struck him that it was sacrilege for such a body to be given to a practically decrepit old man for whom the allures of a female body were always insufficient. As he approached she was staring up at the full moon, almost asking her for advice. She took a sip of the champagne which was in her hand and without looking, placed the glass on the balustrade only to see it wobble off and fall the fifteen foot onto the grass. 'Bugger', she said, under her voice, immediately turning to see whether anyone had seen her foolishness, turning straight into the eyes of him. Him whom she had been pondering on whilst gazing at the moon.

'Swear not by the moon, lest thy love should prove likewise variable.'

'Then what will you have me swear by' she replied, continuing the famous quotes from the star crossed lovers.

He was impressed with her reply, but totally disgusted with his opening line. He must be losing his bloody mind, never had he used this nonsense to woo a girl. He usually believed in the direct approach which had served him well enough over the years.

'I'm sorry', he said, 'but that was the most stupid thing to say. I couldn't seem to think what to say to you.'

She had him. 'Ahh, you poor little helpless thing, am I that scary? To a brave young man like you?' Her tone surprised even her, this is how she wanted to be, no longer shy, immediately at ease and even in control.

He took the blow well and dipped his head slightly with wide eyes, holding her gaze, almost like a jolly uncle to a young child that had been ever so slightly impertinent.

'Would you like another, or will you just throw that over the wall as well?'.

'I'd like another, what I'll do with it I've yet to decide.' She was flowing, she was enjoying herself, she did not want him to leave, even to get her the drink.

As he wondered back to find a drink for her, a group of high ranking officers came out onto the balcony. Among them was the general of the 4th Army, General Rawlinson, in all his resplendent wonder showing off countless medals won for indescribable valour whilst sitting behind a fine antique desk. Although Billy did not realise it, it was him and his friend, Mr Hague who were directly responsible for the deaths of his friends.

'Hello there my dear', Melissa was well known to him through her husband.

'Good evening General, my you do look dashing tonight. Mrs Rawlinson should keep her eye on you'. She suddenly had immense inner confidence, such that she had not experienced before, but there were many emotions on that balmy summer's evening that she had hardly encountered in her short, rather uneventful life.

The old fool chuckled, enjoying her flattery as well as the effect it was having on his colleagues.

'General Rawlinson Sir, there is a despatch at the main door for you Sir'. They both turned to see Billy holding two drinks, telling awful lies, wanting to get the old man away.

'Thank you Captain, excuse me my dear, do not go away, I must hear more of this'

His colleagues followed him out, holding on to the pretence that anything of any importance must include them.

'That's better' he said handing her a drink and staring into her beautiful green eyes. It was her turn to be taken somewhat a back. She was amazed at his impropriety.

'I thought he might ask you to dance, and, well the way you dance would not have done him any good at all'.

She put her mouth up to his left ear and whispered 'I don't dance like that with everyone'. Pulling her head back she again gave him that radiant smile which he returned. Something was happening here.

It was so unconventional. He had acted with an unutterably low decorum when he thrust his thigh between her legs when they danced. She should have been insulted but wasn't. She should be speaking in formal terms to one she hardly knew, but she wasn't. As a married woman she should be ignoring any thinly veiled advances, but she wasn't. This was different, much different. She was truly intrigued by this man, wanted to know all about him. Wanting to know why practically every one of his brother officers wanted his company. Why there was laughter and frivolity wherever he was, for that is what her life lacked. Fun was an activity she had discarded as a very young girl.

The noble General and his entourage were back. 'No such message Captain, what are you doing?'
His entourage were looking similarly intrigued as to the phantom messenger, still oblivious to what anyone else would have immediately realised.

'He was at the door General, although I must say he was a most odd fellow. He asked for General Ronnie Rawlinson which I felt was awful bad form'. He continued 'he also had the largest feet I've ever seen, but peculiarly small hands, I'll try to find him right away General and find out what he's up to.'

She had turned her head immediately he had started, trying her utmost not to let them see her laugh. She was laughing as she remembered laughing at school, but trying to suppress it as a school mistress gazed directly at her. The only way to disguise her laughter was to create a cough, which soon turned to a choking fit. The gallant gentleman came to her aid, but she assured them all that was required was a drink of water as she took her self away to the ladies room.

They met again under the stairs. 'Tell me Captain, have you found the man you seek?'

He turned again to see her smile as he slowly shook his head while joining her mutually understanding smile. 'I must go I'm afraid as I see Colonel Price has joined the general and he hates me'. Her raised eyes suggested a question as to why.

'We served together in France and let's say I know his worth. He's been on the staff ever since', he commented as he kept his eyes on the colonel.

'If you do not object madam, I shall find occasion to see you again'

'I'm sure we'll see each other around the camp.'

'I'll make a point of it.'

He left her with a smile and she held his gaze. He turned away but turned back to say 'Amazingly I could not find my man'. With a smirkish grin he left the house.

'Amazingly I just have', she said to herself and turned away.

She made her way up the central staircase as he left and came to a large window looking out over the drive way where the cars were parked with the chauffeurs congregating and discussing overheard titbits. Then out he came. A captain would not warrant one of these cars, yet he headed straight for the most impressive vehicle and, after a short conversation with the confused looking driver, he jumped in the car and it drove him away. So cheeky, she thought, but Oh how lovely. The smile came back to her face as she watched the car disappear into the night. But what a night!

Chapter 22

It was with much trepidation that Melissa approached the coach house. He had given full details of where he would be waiting in the letter that Melissa had received. After reading it many times she finally confided in Michele who advised her to go. Good old Michele, knows a bit about real life she does! It was outrageous that he had written. How would he know where to find her, to what address to use, how to ensure that nobody, especially the General, would find it first. What an insane risk, how foolish, how compromising, how daring, how nice. His letter started by apologising for the impertinence of its very existence. He went on to say that he had been asked to attend a course on new creeping barrage tactics with some members of the Brigade at the military installation in Dorking. Knowing, somehow, that Melissa spent most of her time at the house in Epsom, he had commented on how nice it would be to be so close to her. He went on to say that he knew the area rather well as he would occasionally visit his Mother's sister who lived there when he was a child. It would be easy for him to break away from the irrelevant course and take a walk by the river that he knew quite well. If the weather was suitable, perhaps they could reduce the distance between them further and he would be waiting by the coach house outside a feature known as the stepping stones at 11.00am. Perhaps she would walk with him for a while. Of course he understood if Melissa found the idea ridiculous and again apologised. He hoped she was well and again thanked her for the dance. He wished he could have stayed at the party longer and went on to say how truly lovely she had looked. He explained how he had thought of very little else since their meeting and went on to say how lovely the walk was around Box Hill and how nice it would be if she could find any way to join him.

The letter had changed something in her. Her heart had pounded as she read every word and she was excited that her affection seemed to be reciprocated. A chance to see him again, a chance to actually be alone with him for a while. A chance to learn more about him. A week had not passed since their meeting and a week would not pass before their putative arrangement. Every hour seemed to take a day, but on the morning Melissa awoke early and was prepared in her mind for the encounter. Michele had told the driver that they both wished to practise driving and as such would be taking the car for a drive on that morning. Melissa knew the stepping stones well. She had played there also as a child and her heart thumped again as they covered the several miles between Epsom and their destination, it was not Michele's awful driving that caused it.

Melissa had thought long and hard about her dress. She decided on the slightly daring calf length dress with her favourite Gibson tuck blouse with small rose embroidery. Both in brilliant white with a wide brimmed hat with roses at the front side with a white linen ribbon which encircled the flowers. It was about as elegant a hat as any woman would have had possession of in England. Her shoes were from Bond Street and would probably be ruined by the walk, but goodness they were pretty, replete with embroidered roses again around them. Clothes were always her thing, from her childhood she knew what worked and what patently didn't. Today she looked good, Michele had told her she had never looked better and she believed her. With a dash of her French perfume which Melissa had bought herself on account of never receiving such things from her fool of a husband. The thought of his shortcomings in that department was the only thought afforded to her husband that day.

Michele had given Melissa her best wishes and had parked the car some hundred yards from the entrance to the rendezvous. Melissa knew Michele would be there for the entire time offering refuge should this whole enterprise prove to be a big mistake.

The morning broke to intense summer sunshine. It would

be a hot one, even for August and the addition of her summer brolly was essential.

Lady Melissa Wilton was as such presented as she walked down the dusty track which separated the coach house from the main road, deliberately fifteen minutes late. And there he stood. Smoking a cigarette, leaning against a tree, seemingly completely confident that Melissa would appear. He was dressed in field uniform, but with every braid where it should have been. His uniformed was adorned with brightly coloured ribbons which represented the medals he had won. Mercer wore these mainly to break up the monotony of his khaki coloured uniform and whereas they did look fine, the significance of the valour he was supposed to have shown was lost on Billy. That aspect was nonsense in his eyes.

As soon as her eyes met him she was again struck with how incredibly attractive he was, better even than she had remembered. He had no hat, his thick light brown hair, longer than was custom for the army, hanging to his collar, falling across his face, combed back behind his ears. His pips on his shoulders gleaming in the summer sun.

He immediately sprang to attention upon hearing her approach and walked towards her with the widest of childlike grins upon his face. He looked extremely healthy with a tanned hue to his face. He approached her, took her gloved hand and kissed it.

'Lady Wilton, thank you so much for coming.' He lied when he continued with 'I did not think you'd come'

An element of formality was in his voice and he felt extremely nervous about this encounter. For the first time he could remember, he actually felt very anxious in the company of this beautiful lady, and was unsure whether any word coming from his mouth would make any sense at all. He could feel his pulse racing in his veins as he was again in the company of the most beautiful and loveable girl he had ever seen. He wanted this girl so much and was determined to act in the way that was necessary for this to happen. He did not know that his best chance was not to act in any other way than his usual normal way. He did not know that this lady was already in love with him, most desperately. All initial discussions between the two would be merely a game.

'Captain, I must tell you that I don't think I will be able to walk with you today, but I had no way of letting you know. It is an impossible idea and I must return very soon.'

Billy looked closely at her and realised this lady was not dressed to merely get back in her car and leave. Melissa had, he correctly thought, every intention of walking with him.

'I understand Lady Wilton.' He felt very uncomfortable calling her that 'and I apologise again for the letter.'

'You can call me Melissa,' she smiled, 'and I do think it was a bold act on your part and I don't know what to make of it.'

'Can we walk just down to the river as you are here, I'll let you go then I promise.'

'It's not up to you to let me go! I'll come and go as I please, Captain Mercer.'

He was pleased she remembered his name, as he had made no mention of it on his letter.

'Well then will you come? Or go?'

He is infuriating. In a way. She thought.

He held her hand, 'Do come, you don't know what it would mean to me.' He looked sincere, truly sincere. And there it was again his childish smile. How could she resist. That was a question for another time for she would not be resisting today.

Her smile was his answer and her confident forward steps his confirmation, as the two began to walk towards the river. And they continued to walk, and walk until over an hour had passed.

'I loved this place as a boy, it seemed so far from London with so much to do. I remember there was a rope swing over the river along here somewhere. I would spend all day swinging with my cousin, not allowing any other boys to have a go.' He smiled to himself as if in on a private joke. 'Long summer days, long before this madness.'

The water was gushing very fast over this stretch of the river making a sound of its own. Melissa told him how she spent her summers as a schoolgirl and how difficult it was to be the daughter of an officer at that time. How she missed her childhood so much, how fed up she was at being sensible all the time.

'Well that is where I come in', he clasped her hand with those words and she looked at him and smiled. How handsome he was close up. How his eyes seemed so bright, yet somewhere there was a sadness which was hard to trace. Melissa asked him so many questions about his childhood and the war and how he managed to get so deeply caught up in it. She asked if he had lost many friends and he answered that he had, he had lost many dear, dear friends. He went on to tell tales of each of them as she roared with laughter, demanding more stories. He now had her arm in his as he demanded one story from her before he would tell her one of his. Another hour passed as they walked and he looked deep into her eyes as he spoke. He did not want to look anywhere else. There was a feeling, the likes of which he had never known. It was as though there were tiny people dancing inside him when he looked at her face. The moment was broken by the sight of an old rope descending from a tree that overhung a deep pool of the river.

'My God there it is! Still there'. He ran up to it, leaned perilously over to grasp it and pulled it to the bank. It had a log tied to the bottom and the children of Dorking were still using the swing. He pulled on the rope a number of times to test its integrity then boldly announced that he would have a swing for old times' sake.

'You can't do that Billy, you're a captain'. Melissa put her hand to her mouth as she surveyed the ludicrous sight before her of him manoevouring his legs around the branch.

'If that means I cannot swing on this rope then I shall resign my commission' he said in a preposterously posh accent, and with a beaming smile he let himself go to swing the thirty feet out over the deep river. Melissa giggled like a school girl as he screamed mid swing 'It still gives me a stomachy after all this time'. A strange word but Melissa knew what he meant. As the pendulum reversed he came flying back towards her, blew her a kiss as he began his journey again over the river. Upon returning he clumsily removed himself from the swing, almost inadvertently swinging out again and fell in the dusty dirt, holding onto the rope.

'Your turn.'

'There is no way you'll catch me on that old thing. The rope will break surely.'

'No it won't', he stressed 'It'd take two of us'. He paused and Melissa knew what was coming. 'What a good idea' he answered.

'No, no no.' Melissa pleaded but it was no use, as Billy was already holding the log at the bottom of the rope and positioning himself on. Secretly she wanted a go, of course she did and finally gave way to Billy's joy, as he was close to accepting defeat.

He was on the swing and lifted her awkwardly trying as best he could to keep one foot on the ground to prevent a premature departure. He lifted her up and placed her so she straddled him in a most unladylike fashion. They were now face to face. He could smell her perfume and feel her sweet breath on his face for a brief moment, and then they were gone. Her stomach felt a similar feeling as the pair accelerated into thin air, leaving the bank and swinging in a fine arc over the water until they were some twenty feet above it. At the extreme end of the swing there was a creak, the rope seemed to lower, followed by a loud and violent snap as the old rope finally surrendered to the weight it was forced to bear. Billy and Melissa found themselves in mid air, but falling vertically down, no longer in a horizontal direction. The log still beneath Billy, both locked together, with a shrill scream directly into Billy's ear, Melissa held on tighter to him as they both plunged towards the torrid water below.

Melissa panicked as she entered the water with an almighty splash entwined with Billy's body. They both sank deep into the water and for a moment Melissa had no breath as the cold water defied the heat of this hot summer day. Before she knew it she was pulled up so her face was clear as Billy carried her away. The water was up to his chest but the current was fairly strong, trying to take them both down stream. Billy was already laughing, but Melissa was not yet ready to see the humour of the situation as their safety was still her main concern. But she was safe, of course she was, safe with him. He wilfully thrust his way through the current, holding her tight until the water was as shallow as their knees and then climbed what was now a slippery bank.

Melissa miraculously was still wearing her hat, which now resembled a soggy pancake and her shoes were ruined, being sodden and now full of mud. Melissa said not a word, nor made a sound as Billy, still laughing, helped her up the bank and into the grassy meadow where they both fell onto the ground. Billy looked at her to be sure she was not furious at him and he liked what he saw in her eyes. Within a second Melissa broke into laughter again as they both lay on the grass with their faces to the sun, chuckling away like children. Through the laughter Melissa managed to say 'I saw your face as we were falling, a frightened little face of a brave officer' they both now roared as the log attached to a small length of rope floated on down the river.

'Nice hat' he remarked as he took off her ridiculous looking hat and poured the remaining contents over her head. In reply Melissa shook her soaked hair into his face, trying to pin his arms down as she did so.

They both fell back again in a mutual hysteria as Melissa moaned about how cold the water was. It was so hot on this August day that the coldness did not last. Billy took off his soaked wool tunic, but Melissa could not divest herself of anything as her white attire became transparent in places, compelling her to continue to lie down.

'The sun will dry us off in no time', he checked the right pocket of his trousers. 'Here' he said as he discovered a stickleback which he had somehow managed to catch during their maritime adventure. This sight was met with more howls of laughter from both of them as Billy threw the unfortunate tiny fish the ten yards back into the river.

There they lay and began to talk again when the laughter finally ceased.

When they had finished relaying their own accounts of their soaking, the conversation again turned to the war and Melissa pressed him further on the conduct of it.

'Are most of them out there fighting for their country, is that the reason?' This aspect did fascinate her.

'None that I have met. A lot perhaps joined for that reason but that is soon lost on them when they reach the front. It's a situation that they find themselves in and just have to deal with because there is no way out of it, may as well make the most of it. Most lads just want to survive and get through it. There are no mighty heroics as the papers have you believe, medals are mostly given to the undeserving. For me, the medals should go to any soldier who lived under an artillery bombardment for any length of time. Myself and Eddie were bombarded for not even five hours once and we all nearly went bloody mad, but some lads have lived under that for two days! I don't know how anyone can do that and not go bloody crackers. It is so loud and intense and violent' He paused, half smiled and looked at her. 'Difficult to explain really. All my friends just wanted to get home, Eddie especially' He had talked of Eddie during their walk and Melissa knew that this man held a very special place in Billy's heart. He looked at the grass, pulled up a few shoots and threw them away at he thought of his old friend again. 'He felt so guilty towards his family because he had changed so much and was scornful to them when he last saw them. He never wrote to them and I know they couldn't understand why. He just wanted to get it over with, go home, make them proud and start again where he left off with them before the war.'

Billy's voice croaked as he looked to the sky.

'He was such a lovely chap, they were all so proud of him. If only I had got him through, got back. They'd have understood eventually I know they would. But he did find it so hard Melissa, he put a brave face on it all the time but he was really struggling. He didn't want to kill anyone, he shouldn't have bloody well been there in the first place. It was so hard having to do that, then having to do it again and again. Once you've killed someone you can never be the same person again.'

He thought again of that time. That time he held Eddie in his arms, Eddie with half his body blown away. Eddie looking to him as though he could somehow help. O God!

He turned to her with tears welling in his eyes which he quickly wiped away, but his voice involuntarily turned to that of a crying child's as he stressed how sorry he was to be breaking up in this way and asked what she must make of him and acted truly embarrassed by it all.

'There is a song that they always sing over there. It goes "we're here because we're here because we're here because we're here" '.

He sang the words to the tune of Auld Lang Syne. 'At first I thought it was bloody stupid but I now know what it's about'. He stopped talking for a while and looked at her with a pained and embarrassed smile.

'You've probably never heard anyone talk like this. I'm sorry but there are so few people back here who have the faintest idea what's going on over there. Everything we have ever been taught as children or any other time about compassion or humility or being a member of civilised society has to be forgotten'.

He lay back down on the grass, eyes again to the sky. He was angry at himself for mentioning such things. Melissa, crouched on her elbow was struck with a feeling of pity, pity for all the men out there. Again there was silence between them, a silence which had a power that flattered its duration.

Melissa took his hand and smiled sweetly in his face.

'I'll be alright in a minute. I'm so sorry, you don't need this nonsense'.

'It's better than being dumped in the river' she tenderly replied, not taking her eyes off him. They both lay back onto the grass, partially dry by now but looking up into the sky, at the clouds passing by, until their eyes were blurred and they felt strangely dizzy by looking up into space. They lay there together and he took her hand in his and there they remained on this beautiful summer day. Together, as they should always be from now onwards.

Billy was suddenly startled by the realisation that they had not eaten. He suggested they walk on to a pub named the Hand in Hand. There they were met by a pleasant landlord who welcomed them in to the dark room which contrasted heavily with the brightness outside. He was still rather damp while Melissa had dried almost completely although there was a nasty greenish watermark running down her elegant blouse. Billy's wool tunic still contained much water, but this was the usual condition in the trenches and he recalled the heavy nature of his uniform when sodden and worn during active service when it was so difficult to get dry. The darkness of the pub contained many couples who were enjoying this summer day at Box Hill as couples had for countless generations. Half the men in here were in uniform, but many were not and Billy could not understand what contribution these people would be making to the war on a week day in the local pub.

Usually there would be no ladies in a pub, but the war seemed to have changed these things and both were aware what the drunken giggling couples would be doing when they walked into the woods which were positioned close by.

They found an empty table in the corner, close to the end of the bar. The table had no cloth on and had scratches inscribed on its surface, many expletives that they both pretended they had not seen. The barman brought them a bottle of wine and a glass of beer. This was not a nice pub a bit of a local's place really and the house speciality was the landlord's wife's homemade pies. They ate and drank and talked more of him but more of her. They learned all that they wanted to learn about each other drank more together as they moved closer, until their thighs and shoulders were touching. Their voices were now so quiet. This tranquillity was abruptly broken by a peanut that arrived on the table between them and bounced away.

Billy turned to see two figures in civilian clothes sitting at the bar. Billy had heard their conversation, both had been drafted but recently had left the army and were now free men. Must have been some kind of useless fuckers to get released from the army at this time! He did not like them even before the arrival of the peanut.

'Sorry pal. Oh sorry captain'

Billy looked slowly at them. 'Alright lads, not to worry aye.'

This was not the accent they expected from a captain, but they knew enlisted men who made captain usually had a compelling reason for such promotion.

He returned to his conversation with a rather concerned Melissa but there was no concern with Billy. Again they were interrupted by a tiny missile which hit him on his shoulder.

Billy turned again, this time to the landlord asking for the bill. Another peanut came over.

'So sorry SIR,' they yelled in drunken giggles to accompany their drunken acts.

An awkward landlord arrived with the bill, he seemed unprepared to deal with the drunken hooligans clutching each other at the bar and laughing.

Billy took some notes from his pocket and handed them to the man.

'They're slightly damp I'm afraid' he said to the puzzled landlord.

'Let's go Melissa' he said as he stood up

'That's right Captain, fuck off. Fucking officers, you made my life a misery you bastards'

Melissa and Billy walked out of the darkness to a barrage of nuts thrown through the air at both of them, some hitting Melissa. As they entered the daylight Billy turned to her and said. 'I am so sorry about that, so sorry darling.'

Melissa was slightly surprised by Billy's reluctance to engage these drunks. A little disappointed in reality but realised it was for the best. As they walked down the hill Billy acted as if the incident had not happened at all. Perhaps such small things meant nothing to him. They briefly discussed the meal, the pub. He held her hand in his as they walked.

They advanced some two hundred yards with the incident in the pub forgotten when Billy suddenly stopped. 'I've left my key in the pub. Sorry darling, would you wait here just a moment while I nip back and get it?'

He was gone before she could answer as he started to gently run back towards the pub. She watched him as he ran, fit and able as he disappeared into the darkness of the Hand in Hand. She turned away, wondering what reaction he would get, slightly concerned for him. She looked up into the beautiful sky for a while and returned her eyes to the door from which he still had not come. Melissa started to walk back when out he came in a calm and dignified manner. He started to run to her, holding up a key as he approached. Despite his running he was not out of breath as he took her arm and they continued their walk away from the pub. They smiled at each other and said not a word. Melissa took his hand in hers and held it to her mouth and kissed it while looking in his eyes. His hand tasted salty. As Melissa looked at it she found it covered in blood, with some bruises already appearing. She stopped, took his other hand and examined it to find the same. When looking at his face again Melissa detected a slight redness and swelling above his left eye, but the damage to his hands was far worse. With a knowing grin she looked back at him and he smiled like a naughty boy. No words were said, but Melissa put her arm in his and held him tight. Tighter than she had held him before. Melissa had never been in the company of a man like this before. Nothing like this at all!

Before long they arrived back at the point where they had to part. They were at the coach house again where they had met some five hours prior. What a day it had been, how mutual was the enjoyment.

'I'm sorry I got you so wet'. He stopped turned and looked into her gorgeous eyes. His heart actually seemed to skip a beat. Melissa shot him another childish grin. He looked to the sky smiling.

'Thank you so much for today. I think this has been the finest day ever. He paused, 'because of you, you lovely girl.' He took her hand and kissed it passionately. He then put each hand on each of her blushed cheeks and pulled her gently towards him. Without seeking reciprocation he leaned close to her, pausing just as he was close to her lips, then advancing, making contact with them. At that moment he felt as though the ground beneath him slightly gave way and inside he had a curious sensation, like a startled canary flapping in an inadequately sized cage. Melissa's frozen face thawed as every action of his lips and mouth was followed by her as her arms crept around his waist and up to his shoulders. The kiss lasted some moments, he then broke away, keeping his face almost touching hers. They both smiled from such close range. The kind of smiles you only occasionally see. Smiles of those in love. Totally and completely in love.

Melissa broke their embrace and walked to the car, waving her hand. He stood planted in the spot staring at her face. Then she was gone.

Billy returned to his unit that evening, having taken the long walk back. His mind was spinning and he could not prevent himself from grinning inanely like a silly child. Everything about this girl was just perfect. Here beauty now seemed the least of her qualities. Her smell, her softness, her occasional childishness and her fiery temperament. He liked the questions she had asked him, he enjoyed answering them.

She seemed different to how she had been at the Ball, but in a better way. He experienced the serious side to her nature and was moved by her tenderness in his weak moment. He felt the dampness in the bottom of his pocket as he laughed out loud while walking back. He knew, without doubt, that his life would never be the same.

The course lasted just one more morning and he was back to Brigade headquarters, now thirty miles back from the front. There was no means of escape on this final day as his absence was duly noted for the previous day. The lectures on the merits of the creeping barrage with shock troop infantry tactics was really quite enlightening and this was the only topic of conversation during the coach ride and two train journeys to the coast. Billy was not the most vocal in these particular discussions. He was content to gaze out of the windows at the Surrey countryside, his mind elsewhere.

Chapter 23

He was back at his desk the following day when the General first mentioned the Brigade assault he was planning. They were to take a small section of higher ground from which they could then be involved in the final push that was to come later. Billy was alarmed to notice at once that this was ground he knew well. He had been stationed in this sector of the trench when he served with Eddie and knew how difficult it was to defend. Launching an attack from here would be madness, especially in isolation. If there were to be a big push at Divisional or Corps level, the heavily guarded German defence would be distracted on other sectors, but an isolated attack would be met with the full force of this robust defence. He knew that this higher ground housed a dozen machine gun posts which were completely hidden by the topography of the ground. This particular sector was so precarious that the British had not been able to retrieve their dead from unsuccessful trench raids. These raids had supplied Brigade with the information that the defences were practically impregnable. This would be carnage. Two thousand men attacking this position would be the work of a complete lunatic.

Billy took the papers over to Wilton who was joined by Price, again drinking a fine whisky.

'Mercer! Nice to see you. How was the course?' Wilton was as jovial as ever.

'Fine sir, thank you. Sir I've seen the plans for this new attack. I know this ground sir. I was there for some weeks. I really think you should analyse it before authorising this attack. The ground there is very wet due to the river and the trenches too shallow. The Hun will know we are amassing. I think it will be a mistake. I was looking at the aerial photographs and we could launch a similar attack on slightly higher ground at the other side of Moreuil and come back on ourselves to secure that ground. To take it straight on would just not be possible sir.'

'General Debeney wants to launch the offensive there Mercer and it would be better to launch the push from the German trench not the low ground we have now. We must take it Mercer and it would be quicker to take it directly. Don't worry Mercer, I'll organise a large Bombardment, all the wire will be cut. We must take it.' The General was enjoying discussing his plan.

'I know sir, we could take it but not from there. Can we go over and take a look sir, you will agree with me immediately once you see the ground.'

'We have examined the ground and the attack will proceed at all costs Mercer.' Price interjected.

'They will all be massacred there sir, please let me show you. We have been bombarding that position for years, the ground just gives too much protection from a frontal assault. Please sir, too many will die in this'

'Mercer, that is quite enough. Do not presume to tell the General how to conduct a battle. You forget yourself Mercer' Colonel Price said, desperate to involve himself.

'I can't forget what I have seen in that sector Colonel,' replied Billy.

'You must show more fighting spirit Mercer. We have well trained troops there, your old battalion for one. The Royal Scots are there spoiling for a fight. I have seen the full plans and I advised the general to go ahead. The Germans will capitulate I assure you'.

'No Colonel Price, you are wrong. You are so wrong'

'Go now Mercer, get out. Just you make sure the ammunition is brought up the line in time, we go in five days.'

Mercer tried again to object but was met with a hysterical scream from Price. He looked deep into the Colonel's eyes, almost behind them and turned and left the room, closing the door behind him. He headed straight for his room and a bottle of whisky that was full but within a couple of hours would be completely empty.

The next two days was taken up with logistical calculations, but Mercer was preoccupied with thoughts of all the men he knew from the 9th Battalion who would be taking part in this futile assault. He had not seen Wilton or Price during this time but was requested to report to Price the following morning.

He entered the Colonel's grand office and noticed Brigadier General Wilton standing by the seated Colonel. 'Stand there would you Mercer.' The Colonel barked at him expecting him to stand in front of the desk like a private addressing his subaltern.

'Mercer we have had a report from England of a very serious nature. It appears that you failed to attend the second day of the artillery course. Is that true?'

'Yes Sir.'

'Well, it appears that on that day in question, a Fusilier Captain assaulted two men in the Hand in Hand pub. One of the men, a Mr Ramsden required hospital treatment for broken nose, jaw and loss of eight teeth. It was apparently a frenzied attack and the captain in question did not stop even after the man lost consciousness. The landlord of the pub went straight to the training unit with a description which was very close to you Mercer. Well it is now a police matter and they want you to return to discuss this.'

Billy was pleased at this news, another chance to see her.

'Was it you Mercer who attacked these people?'

'Yes Sir, yes it was.'

The Colonel glanced at Wilton who bowed and shook his head in genuine disappointment.

'Right! Well I have another question. Were you alone Mercer?'

Billy was instantly stunned. He answered with silence.

'Were you alone?' he screamed, almost making Billy jump. Still no answer.

'The landlord a Mr, eh..' he checked some paperwork beneath him,

'Mr Conby stated that the Captain in question was with a woman who he described as very attractive and aged in her twenties. He recalled her name as Melissa. The General here has since spoken to his driver who told him that his wife and her maid, who has now lost her situation, took the car out that day.'

Billy retained his silence but was screaming inside. He knew now the problems he had caused everyone by his recklessness. He stood before the two senior officers with his hands behind his back, feeling like a private. The General also had his eyes down, broken hearted by these events.

'Mercer, not only have you committed a serious criminal act, you have broken the code of a British officer in a most egregious manner. You are an absolute disgrace to your regiment and to the whole army.'

The Colonel was seemingly enjoying every minute of this. It was unbearable for Wilton who stepped away to look out of the French windows. Mercer retained his composure practically dying inside.

'Can you explain exactly what you were doing with the General's wife involved in a bar room brawl.'

'No Sir, no I cannot.' Meaning he would not discuss this. It was difficult enough without unnecessary words augmenting the situation. He glanced briefly at the General who continued to survey the gardens.

'Do you presume to cuckold a General Mercer?' More unnecessary embarrassment for the hapless Wilton.

'You should be turned over to the civil police and should lose your commission with your regiment Mercer. But we have decided upon a different course of action. We have replied to the police force that you cannot be returned as you will be leading an offensive within the next few days. You are to rejoin your regiment immediately and will not be welcome at the general staff again. If you have so much knowledge of these positions as you claim, then you just may be an asset with the push. You are to retain your rank for the purpose of this attack and will be demoted after that time. You are to lead B Company on the assault which will include your old platoon.'

This was a tremendous blow to Billy, but he understood. His punishment for his indiscretion was therefore probable death, without a chance of seeing her again. That was the hardest to bear. It was a neat solution. There could hardly be a scandal if one part of it was dead.

'You know that attack is futile Colonel, you know what sending me back means.'

'Nonsense Mercer, you will take those trenches and any defeatist talk like that in front of your men will be regarded as cowardice in the face of the enemy.'

'Cowardice Sir?' they both understood fully what he meant. Price continued.

'Now, I would like you to leave tomorrow morning and take the full plans to the other Captains. You are to brief them all so please take time to analyse the plans and the timings of the artillery support. Now get out of my sight'

'Out of *your* sight Sir?' this presumptuous twat, when it was the General who was feeling the brunt of Billy's actions. Billy saluted them both, turned and left the room.

'I will be returning home to the house in Epsom to see my wife Colonel.' The General spoke in a soft tone. 'I will leave immediately and I would like you to come back personally and tell me the result of the push please.' He felt betrayed and hurt by his humiliation and had not liked the glee that Price seemed to derive from it.

'We will not be seeing Mercer again Colonel which I am sure will cheer you up.' Wilton had not moved from his position by the windows. He finally moved and turned to leave, finding the gaze of Price. 'Regardless of this all, he is a better man than you Price' He walked past the desk of Price and reached the door, taking the polished brass handle that was slippery to the touch. While facing the still closed door he said 'Wasted love.' He opened the door, walked half way through, turned to Price again and said in a louder and more emotional way. 'Wasted love.' Then slammed the door shut behind him. Price stared at the door in bemusement.

Billy was at his desk collecting some of the very few personal effects that were contained therein. His mood was very low. He thought he had escaped the war, thought he would see it through. He had found a woman that he was deeply in love with and he had his life mapped out. He would sell his wine, generate some funds and elope with Melissa. He knew this war was drawing to a close. Having been party to some sensitive information, he knew that Germany was finished. One last push would be enough now that the German Spring offensive had ended in failure. He just needed to sit out the war, get demobilised, take his love and live in happiness for the only time in his life. He was so close to his master plan.

But not now. He had ruined it for himself. Attacking those two fools in the Hand in Hand was his mistake. He would have avoided this show if he had not done that. It had now cumulated in this. Sent back to the front. Sent on a Brigade offensive that could only fail. A worthless assault which had no chance of success. An advance into, what would appear to be, certain death. Billy had every reason to be despondent.

His orders were to depart on this morning and he would be with his old regiment by the evening.

He was pained by the thought that he would not be able to let Melissa know. He could well be dead before she would know he was no longer on the staff. Using all his ingenuity would not help him on this one. There was just no conceivable way getting to her. Letters to her now would be surely read. He considered one to her maid Michele, but rejected the idea as he did not know whether she was aware of things despite driving her to Dorking. If only he had asked Melissa whether Michele was compliant in their enterprise that day. But he had not, so he could not take that risk. He had caused Melissa enough trouble.

He was going back into Hell and was unsure whether he would be able to stand it. His nerves had been so shattered by his experiences there and he had no desire to return at all. He was in danger of collapsing or doing something stupid and the uncertainty was causing him grave concern. He was in a dark place in his mind at that moment.

There was a knock on his door, which then opened. He turned to see the sight of Colonel Price, the one man he did not want to see at this moment and he was unsure whether he would be able to restrain himself.

'Captain Mercer.' That made a change from the usual bellowed 'Mercer' he was used to. Billy did not acknowledge his presence.

'Captain Mercer, I wonder if we could have a talk.' Still nothing from the younger man. Price viewed him collecting desk objects and placing them in an old box. 'Captain I am fully aware what you think of me, but I thought I would just wish you well.' Mercer looked up in surprise and then continued his work.

'I was looking through your record and noticed that you took part in the assault on High Wood with the 20th Battalion in '16. That was a rough show and I was due to lead that assault but didn't. I rather got the wind up Mercer I'm afraid and felt I could not do it. What I am trying to say is that you must have known that fact but never mentioned it to anybody. Despite all our differences, my, well, actions on that day, hidden from everyone by the one remaining survivor from that day. For all this time I did not realise it was you, only this morning. Well, I want to thank you for that Mercer.' He paused hoping for some response.

'We really did get off on the wrong foot and I believe that could be my fault. I never approved of men coming through the ranks but upon reflection you have been a good man Mercer. I know you have seen the front many times and you have contributed well to our unit here. Well, anyway, that be as it may, God speed to you.'

Mercer continued to ignore Price as he began to see the futility of his task and started to walk out. Just as he reached the door he stopped again.

'Mercer, I think you have all that is good in a British Soldier and I'm proud to have served with you.' He paused as if searching for words 'It's difficult for me you see, working here and organising all these terrible shows. People die because of what we do here and yet I have never been over the top myself. It seems unfair in a way. I'm trying to say I'm sorry for everything and hope we can be better friends when you return.' He gave a half smile hoping for some reciprocation which he did not receive.

Billy finished packing items in the box, picked it up into his arms and walked towards the door to where Price stood. Price was expecting a positive reply and Billy moved as if to speak. Price's eyes rose in expectation and he put out his hand expecting it to be shaken but when Billy got to within a few inches from his face the Colonel finally got his reply.

'Fuck off you old CUNT!'

Price was instantly turned to stone as Billy casually walked passed, out of the door and down the hallway. Price, who was stunned and speechless, was never to see him again.

Chapter 24

It was Billy's belief that, despite his misgivings over the assault and his own situation he must do as best he could for the poor souls who he would be leading in this enterprise. He would be the highest ranking officer who would be taking part in the actual fighting. When he finally returned he visited all Battalion headquarters for the three battalions who would be attacking and the Colonel of the artillery who would be providing support. He detailed all the plans from Brigade HQ and warned them all that this would be no easy task. Each Battalion had a Colonel in command with several Majors or Captains taking charge of the companies which were in turn broken down into their platoons led by Second Lieutenants usually. All these officers were present at his briefings and Billy felt confident that he had conveyed diligently and effectively, the plan devised. Each man knew his role, each Junior Officer or Subaltern as they were known would have their own task of briefing their platoons and Billy in turn would brief his old platoon that he would be leading over the top along with his Subaltern. He began his journey back to the front line to visit his own unit. The closer he came, the louder was the noise and the greater the activity.

After making his way from the relative safety of the communication trench, Mercer passed a guard and entered the reserve trench once more. This was the line where most of their time was spent prior to moving up to the front line for assaults, lookout duty or simply to maintain a presence in the face of the enemy. The young private guarding the mix of wire and wood which formed the gateway from communication to fighting trench saluted Mercer as he passed by. Mercer merely met the salute with a look which told the private how useless such a gesture was to him. Ironically, there was a time when Mercer appreciated and was proud of the nuances of the military, but now it was futile in the face of the mess facing all of them. As he entered the line he almost collided with an Adjutant who'd been up the line delivering confidential orders. His relatively clean uniform irritated Mercer. 'Ahh Mercer, there you are, where have you been, I've been looking for you.'

'Fuck off Lanson and get out of my fucking way.' Evident to all by these words was the fact that Mercer had slipped into a very fowl disposition and was clearly better left alone.

'Now look here', squeaked the highly tuned accented Adjutant, 'That was bloody un called for'. Mercer stopped and slowly caught his eyes. Lanson became increasingly uncomfortable with what was appearing like a stand off between the two 'I've come to deliver orders from Battalion HQ regarding Thursday and would expect a little more respect from you Captain.' He knew he'd said too much. Mercer said slowly and deliberately. 'Now get out of my way you piece of shit before I knock you out. I've just come from Brigade HQ, you self important prick, so I know what you've got in your hand. Just fuck off out of it, now!'

Lanson had no reply to this highly unjustified assault, but to stand at the wall of the trench and look in disbelief. Mercer continued on his journey. He passed the hundred smells that greeted anyone in the trenches and made his way to the dugout for a large swig of the Scotch which he knew was waiting for him. He passed a group of soldiers from a Scottish sounding regiment and approached the familiar sounds of his own company. As he neared another bend, he heard the annoying voice of Sgt Robbins.

He called him and all other Sergeants and NCOs with the junior Officers into his dugout which acted as company HQ to brief them also on the attack. It was from here that he received the most complaints about the attack. These were the men who had lived in this sector and knew, like Billy knew, that this attack was destined to fail. Sgt Robbins especially was vocal in his dislike of the plans that Billy presented. Most of the men who knew Mercer were pleased when they heard he would be returning to the unit, but not Robbins. He had his personal problems with the Captain. Billy managed to put Robbins in his place as he always had done and Billy received a look from Robbins that suggested there would be as much danger to Billy coming from Robbins's revolver as German hardware.

The attack was to take place in two days time, the lads would be going over at 5.30 pm as it was thought that the afternoon sun would be in the defenders eyes. The plans mentioned most gaily that the assaulting troops would have their shadows in front of them as the sun obscures the German. Utter tosh of course, this would make little difference.

Billy was slightly surprised by Robbins's objections. Although this man was a bully and felt he was in command of his platoon, he always did have fighting spirit in abundance and was usually eager for an attack. Billy dismissed them all, leaving it to the Sergeants to explain the plan to the troops on the morning of the assault. The less time they had knowing the plans the better, as, if one was to be taken in a trench raid, he would give away the details. The Germans had launched many such raids recently, suspecting some event.

The briefing complete, Billy asked his batman to make his dinner while he opened a bottle of whisky and laid on his bunk facing the ceiling, enjoying the opportunity to be alone for a while as all else were out on duties. The whisky tasted good and as he lay there his thoughts immediately turned to her. He smiled to himself and he was comforted with the picture of her in his mind. He was back to a better place, a place where he loved and was loved in return. In a sense it pained him to think that this angel of a woman actually loved him too. Incredible, to be loved by one such as her who would be now waiting for some contact from him. With these thoughts on his mind he sank into a deep and restful sleep. His batman had to throw his dinner away as the other officers ate the fine meal while their captain slept beside them.

He awoke in the dead of night with a jolt. He had been dreaming of her. So vivid and real. He felt his heart was bleeding for her. He even had silly notions to talk to somebody about her. But he had no friends here now. No-one like Eddie. How he wished he was here too. He could talk to him all day about these things. He said out loud to himself as he lay on his bed thinking of Eddie for a moment. 'I wish you were with me now. But… I don't suppose that's going to happen'. A fellow officer moved in his bed as he spoke. Billy sat up to find his fellow officers sleeping. He decided to get up and view trenches where they would be setting off from on the evening of the following day. With her on his mind he stood up and walked out of the mud walled dug out into the balmy warmth of this summer night. He was greeted with the smell of cooking, as he passed a small section of troops frying their Bully Beef in an attempt to soften it. His mind returned to the KRP and how he would tuck into his supplies in the dead of night and they would all share his hampers from Fortnum and Mason. He had to try to dispel these thoughts. They would drive him insane, but recently awoken minds do seem to jump around in such fashion.

A soldier was looking out over no man's land and Billy approached him asking to look through the periscope. All so quiet out there, a few pieces of broken wire, some decomposed bodies, accounting for the unpleasant smell that pervaded the entire area. Many shell holes, some filled with water despite the summer heat.

'Thank you' he said to the soldier as he walked on inspecting the trench. It was in a bad way, in some places not high enough to walk through without ducking down. Pete would have struggled here he thought. Again, back to the past. Torturing himself.

As he turned a corner of the trench he heard voices. The familiar voice of Sgt Robbins was emerging from the NCO's dugout. A voice which seemed loud even when spoken softly, that harsh tone which would go through a steel sheet. Bloody nuisance of a man, keeping everyone awake with his fog horn of a voice, he thought.

To make mischief, Billy decided to wait outside the dugout

and overhear the conversation, to hear Robbins criticise him.

Robbins was with two corporals and a number of privates, discussing the forthcoming attack. Strictly against the rules as the men should not have been told. Billy could put him on a charge, but what the fuck did he care about military protocol anymore.

He listened to Robbins's words.

'I just wanted to see her, just once. She was born two months ago now and I've had two leaves cancelled in that time.' Robbins was showing rare humility it seemed during this conversation. 'Now we get told of this assault, I don't think I'll ever see her now. I want to see my wife again too. Don't laugh you bastards', but Robbins himself was laughing as was evident in his voice. 'I was a nasty old sod to her before, but since she told me she was having a baby I long to see her. I'm gonna be mister lovely to her now, I know you don't believe me but I will. I am so sick of it out here and it has made me realise how lucky I am at home. Sergeants are always at the end of the line with leave and if they'd let me go last month at least I would have seen them both before I… well, you know.'

'Leave off Sarg, you're not dead yet mate. You'll get through, you'll see them again. This war will be over soon everyone knows it' A cheeky young corporal gave his sanguine opinion.

'Thanks Dayton, but I've just got such a bad feeling about this one. I've never felt it before. I think this is gonna be a real bad one, don't think I'll get through. I just wish I could hold my little girl just once and give her a big kiss and tell the missus that I love her.' His voice began to crack. Billy had never heard him talk like this and felt a compassion for the man he had never liked.

'Not such a hard man after all are you Sarg', the same corporal said. 'I will be with you you little bugger if you keep on,' Said Robbins. 'I'll shoot you if the Hun doesn't.'

The group sniggered and the sound rose up into the starry night as Billy walked past them all. 'Morning sir' a number of them said as they caught sight of him through the entrance of their dugout. 'Morning lads', he said and continued his inspection of the line.

It was just over an hour to stand to which coincided with the dawn. Billy spent this time looking over the entire length of the trench from which they would be going over the top. This filled him with no solace at all. This was going to be a complete bloody disaster.

He then oversaw stand to at dawn and finally returned to his dugout for a nice breakfast. He was starving hungry and needed a drink as well.

After a good feed he called in the officers again to go over the plan again, asking for Robbins to attend. He knew his sergeant had told his men when he shouldn't have done, but still went through the motions of telling him not to divulge the plans to anyone. Robbins convincingly said he would not. Billy dismissed all the men but asked Robbins to remain.

Robbins expected some extra onerous duties to be imposed on him and stood silent, trying not to look at his captain.

'Robbins we are going over the top tomorrow afternoon with a full compliment of fifteen hundred men.'

Robbins looked bored 'Yes I know Sir.'

'All these men have been through a lot together and I think they have a great tale to tell for the regiment. I want somebody to tell their story some day.'

Robbins looked confused.

'I have here the full list of everyone going over. I also have confirmation of all the weapons and ammunition received.'

'Yes Sir'. What could this be about he wondered.

'Robbins, I want you to take these pages back to Divisional HQ in Calais and then go onto the leave that you should have had.'

'But sir...'

'Yes Robbins, I'm afraid you will miss the show tomorrow.'

The Sergeant could not contain his smile as he began to realise what was being proposed. He was to get out of it, he was going home. For a moment he was in love with Captain Mercer!

'We have a full compliment of NCOs and if you are stopped here is my personal permission to leave the line and take your leave. So, go and say goodbye to the lads and be on your way.' Billy was smiling now as he knew what this meant to this man.

Robbins slowly moved out of the dugout, still not quite believing that his dream had come true. As he marched out Billy called 'Sergeant.'

He turned, expecting to be told it was a joke.

'Kiss that little daughter of yours.'

'Yes I will sir. Thank you Sir, thank you so much. Thank you sir' He was beaming now, the happiest man in the world for that moment.

Mercer followed him with his eyes, still smiling. When he was gone Billy's smile turned slowly to a frown as he was hit with a hint of jealousy. If only he was going home. Her face appeared again.

Chapter 25

As he crossed the dugout and fell onto his dilapidated chair, he was overwhelmed with a despondent feeling. If it was him with a warrant to leave the front line. He knew what he would do with it. He would go straight to her. The girl that now was his life. He cursed his own part in his exile that was imposed on him. Things would have been different. They would have worked it out somehow. All the obstacles could have been overcome.

Where there's a will there's a way aye?

But not now. He picked up a half full bottle of whisky that lived under his writing desk. Placing his tin cup in the middle of the table, he poured the liquid increasing the height and in turn increasing the volume of noise as the tin reverberated around the dugout. When the cup was half full he twisted his wrist and stopped the flow, watching as the bubbles in the cup disappeared one by one leaving the now calm whisky in the cup. Down went the bottle, up went the cup and down went the whisky, warming his throat as it went. He looked at the pad of warrants on his desk. So many still there, so much freedom in those innocuous pieces of paper. On his left was an order from the General. He eyed the signature on the bottom. Such a plain signature. So easy to copy.

No there was not time. It was too late. Not enough time. Was there?

Life without Michele was difficult for Melissa. Now there was no-one. No-one who could share a word or even a glance with.

Her husband had returned to the house and missed no opportunity to display the disgust and contempt that he held her in. But Melissa had changed. No longer the obeying and diffident, grateful girl in his presence. No. She was worth more than that and offered him no explanations, nor did he seek them. He reduced himself to gleefully explain that 'Mercer' had been sent back to the front. That he would lead the assault. That it was unlikely that anybody would see him again. How Mercer had been such a disappointment. Yes, to you and your demented motives, absolutely yes, she thought but never gave utterance to such sentiments. The dinner with her husband was as quiet as usual but Melissa did detect a strange expression on his face. He seemed to possess mad looking eyes and it was a profile that had not been seen in Wilton before. Melissa just wanted to be finished, flee to her room which she thankfully did not share with him, get her head on her pillow and cry. It was rather odd, to be eagerly anticipating the opportunity to cry, but that is what Melissa was yearning for. It gave her some comfort as well as the chance to think only of him. Very soon dinner was over and Melissa made some hint of a goodnight salutation and raced up the stairs, fell face first onto her bed and cried. Again. It was going to be another long night another unbearable night wondering where he was, what he was doing and whether he was thinking of her. Eventually her desperate mind gave way to sleep.

With a sudden jolt Melissa awoke. There was a sound. Something below her window. When her attention was greeted with only silence, her head fell back on the damp pillow.

There it was again, a rustling sound from below. Then a voice cursing to itself prior to a loud noise of someone falling. His voice.

It could not be. It must be surreal in the true sense of that word. The noise started again as Melissa jumped out of bed, ran to the window, opened it up, looked below and saw the only sight that could calm her swollen heart. She saw him.

He looked up at her as a thousand questions flew through her head. Was it really him? How did he get here? Had he deserted? He smiled up at her.

'I don't think Romeo had this problem' he said as he attempted another climb up the feeble ivy branches that led to her window. Melissa was in a trance, not able to speak through the shock. He was making such a noise that would surely wake the house, but nobody seemed to respond. Melissa looked at her bedside clock. Two twenty in the morning, not even the servants would be awake.

He had a good footing now and continued his ascent towards her. Then he was there. At her window then through her window then standing before her, in her room, the two of them alone.

There were so many questions to ask. So many explanations. But now was not the time for words. Their mutual longing spurned such things. It was time now to act upon the desires they had both felt since the time they had met.

He approached her and again put both of his palms on her cheeks. There would be no reticence from her, no pretence of a woman's modesty. He put his lips to hers and immediately an intense passion gripped them both. His tongue was deep in her mouth, her tongue responding vigorously. Her mouth felt so small and tender, his so overpowering. Melissa showed no sign of hesitation and started to feel her way over his mighty frame. Being so much smaller, Melissa felt completely enveloped in this man, his musty smell pleasant and adding to her arousal. The need to remove each other's clothes came with haste and, despite Billy's complicated attire, he was soon naked in her arms. Billy displayed his obvious excitement as Melissa dared to lower her eyes. His head came back to her, planting itself between her breasts as he crudely ripped at the buttons of her blouse to reveal her perfectly formed, surprisingly large perfect breasts. Down below he was as hard as any stone and Melissa pressed herself against him again to feel him. His mouth was straight onto her left then right breast, his tongue performing circular movements which turned both her nipples as hard as his bursting manhood. As he sucked away at her Melissa took him in her hand and felt wet between her legs as her fingers squeezed around him. He gasped with pleasure as she began rhythmically running her hand up and down, simulating what would surely follow. Wanting to catch sight of it again, she looked down but Billy picked her up like a baby and carried her over to her bed. As he laid her down he worked at her skirt and soon Melissa was naked but for her underwear which were all that protected her total nakedness. Melissa felt his fingers on the top of her underwear and downward pressure ensured their removal. She gasped as she lay, completely at his mercy, completely open to him to do what he would. He raised himself up to get full view of her gorgeous supple yet firm body. The body of a true woman. He felt capable of exploding on the spot and had to restrain himself. He laid his hands on the thighs and kissed her legs moving up as he did so, up to her thighs. He was possessed with a desire to get his tongue between her legs. As he moved closer, Melissa was suddenly afraid of what would follow. This was an act that she had only ever heard gossip about. His mouth now went ever closer. Melissa recalled a French friend of hers laughing at English men by saying that they thought their tongues were for speaking with. She had laughed thinking she understood at the time, especially when Michele said they should at least speak those Latin terms! Now it was happening, happening to her. He was mere inches away but she could not stop him. This man could do whatever he wished. Then he was there. Melissa was shocked but oh my God, she thought, that feels so good!

He looked at her bedside clock. It was now past four o'clock. What to do Billy? he thought. Melissa was asleep in his arms, occasionally kissing his chest in her slumber. He loved her nakedness beside him, felt as though he was in paradise beside her. How can anyone leave heaven for hell? He kissed her dark hair as he contemplated his next move. It was then that his thoughts turned to the men in those trenches that would be going over the top in under fourteen hours. He held her, breaking her slumber. His chest pushed close to hers, he pressed harder and harder, as if trying to break the barrier between their hearts. With a tender groan that only women can make, Melissa invited him in again and he obliged, moving rhythmically and kissing her mouth. Even at this time he knew he would be going back.

The driver who had brought him to Epsom from Waterloo was still waiting. Handsomely paid, he took him on his return journey. If he could just get to Southampton again he would find any of the numerous transports back over the water and back to the front.

His absence was noted. A wire had been sent to brigade for information and a negative reply was received. There were in total some forty officers taking part all of whom were waiting for their final briefing from Captain Mercer. They were mustered in a Colonel's residence just behind the reserve trench of this sector. The Colonel himself was very concerned, not least by the prospect of appointing a replacement to lead the assault which could in theory have been he. A number of Majors shared this concern as Mercer was now a full hour late for this briefing. Was it possible that he had deserted? Most who knew him doubted this but this was all most peculiar.

There was noise from outside of the bomb ruined house which was their location. A very vocal 'Evening Sir' from a sentry heralded the arrival of an officer. That officer was Captain Mercer.

He had answered her questions. How he had got there, how he would try to get back, what he was soon to be engaged in. He told her he would get through, get home again to her, would always be with her. He told her how she had changed his life, how his mind has been on nothing else since they met. How he loved her, how he truly loved her.

How their life together will be wonderful as she snaked her body around his, kissing him again and making love with him again.

Chapter 26

Five minutes to go. Just time for one more walk by and a worthless pat on the shoulder for those whose terror was almost preventing them standing. The sound of the guns was now thunderous, making one not only cover the ears but perversely squint the eyes with the sound. He walked down the mud filled trench, mud now up to the shins of the awaiting British Infantry. The sergeant had the men lined up correctly with their shaking bayonets emerging from the trench. He resented the sound of these monstrous guns, he wished he could have silence before such an extreme activity that he was about to embark upon. Time to think of his life, think of her, her face, her body, her smell. But the guns wouldn't let him. No.

He had the advantage of having undergone this ordeal before, most of the boys he was walking by had not. Boys he referred to them as, for boys they were. His twenty one years were above the average of this platoon, he knew there were some shockingly younger than permitted. If he had his way he'd send them all back and abort this futile assault which would result in nothing but agonising death for the majority of those he was presently walking by.

'Come on lads, do your best. By breakfast we'll be eating German sausage, just like the French whores over there'. No one heard, no one cared they just mumbled to themselves and continued to shake. To his left he saw Lieutenant Jones slumped against the trench wall, his face white with fear, transfixed on his watch trying with his mind to stop the second hand from ticking. He checked his. Five twenty seven, three minutes left.

As he turned back he noticed Private Walker bawling like a three year old, crying so loudly he could even hear it. He grabbed him from behind and shouted in his ear, his voice no louder to Walker than a whisper.

'When you get over, lie down as soon as you can and

fucking stay there, don't fucking move, you'll be all right. Your Mum will see you soon'. This visibly helped the lad who stood straight but still had tears streaming down his face. The private next to him gazed with wide hypnotised eyes at his officer, not looking directly at him. Mercer nodded to him as if to tell him the same applies.

He patted each one as he walked back to his starting position, one was being sick against the muddy wall of the trench. The sound of the exploding shells had now merged into one mighty roaring sound, much like that of a wave crashing in on a shingle beach. His troops were looking at him for comfort, knowing he'd been through this torture before, elevating him to almost God like status. Knowing what he did was no consolation as he was aware of what faced them when they climbed these ladders in a few seconds and attempted to charge the opposing trench. What faced them then was scarcely worth thinking of.

The falling shells coupled with the rain had turned No man's land into a thick bog, like a primeval soup, only no life would emerge from this, only disappear. Wire, wooden stakes, dead men all stock to add to the dreadful ingredients. Advancing through this would be difficult enough with full packs without being shelled, machine gunned, hand-grenaded and gassed. Mercer now himself began to shake, the uncontrollable involuntary reflex which set into so many soldiers in this position. Ironically some form of physiological defence mechanism. The shakes were running the length of his spine, to his knees making them tremble in an almost amusing manner. He told himself to think of something else as he had these men relying on him, think of something else. Her. There she was again, in her white cotton dress that allowed the sun to shine through on that day in Dorking. The way she looked at him after he'd kissed her before she left. That confident look which he saw for the first time then. The looked that told him she truly, truly loved him, pretence being over. She was his to do with as he would, if circumstances would only allow.

The way she bit his shoulder as she orgasmed for the second time during that encounter just a night previously. The noise she made, like a child, showing him that sex was for loving, not a rough physical, aggressive, self gratifying show of dominance. Sex was almost invented for those two. How he felt part of her and wished to be with her even more directly after the event, when he would usually wish to leave. How she got enjoyment out of his body and him hers. How he broke the woman in her at her bequest. How he loved her, really loved her.

With a muddy finger he wiped clear the glass of his watch, one and a half revolutions of the second hand left. Time to check his revolver, pull the release clasp, check all six rounds in the chambers. He felt inside his tunic pocket for the dozen or so rounds which were surprisingly heavy. He checked the leather cord that attached his revolver to his tunic. On the other leather cord from his right side was his tin whistle which he raised to his mouth. His platoon turned to him awaiting the sound which would signal their advance. 'Take ladders' the sergeant called out as the front man of each section took the creaky wooden structure in both hands. An eight foot climb took them from the relative safety of the trench to Hell.

The thirty foot stretch of trench between the traverses contained his entire platoon, most of whom he had never spoken to. He could see them now mouthing words to hastily spoken prayers to a God of Love. No room for a God of Love here, only the Roman God of the red planet. Along the entire length of the battalion's front men were doing the same. The whole of the Brigade was going over this afternoon. Four platoons to a company, three companies to a battalion, and four battalions to this brigade. Almost one thousand five hundred infantry soldiers going over the top.

But he had seen the plans, he knew the strength of the German defences, he knew the wire would scarcely be cut, he knew the German dugouts would protect them from the artillery barrage, he knew they would be out with their Maxim machine guns and repeating rifles the moment the barrage stopped, he knew the assault would be a complete disaster, again. He knew that by chance he should have fallen by now, he knew that almost all those he served with were dead, he knew he'd been living a charmed life, he knew his luck would run out, soon.

Thirty seconds to go, the overhead bombardment stopped. That'll give them just enough time to get back to their positions he thought. Relative quiet ensued, the prayers and groans of the troops audible over the clattering of kit.

'Remember boys, you're all fucking heroes already, to stand here knowing you're about to do this. The whole country is so proud of you all and so am I. So lets get out there and rip apart these Fritz bastards that have put you through this shit for so long. Lets all fucking ram these bayonets in their fucking throats. Ready for it boys, God bless you all, see you in fucking Berlin.' Words said for his benefit more than theirs.

Ten seconds to go. He took the breath that would be exhaled into the whistle, stepped to his ladder, took hold of it and closed his eyes. There she was again, holding his hand looking at him, 'Please come home.' Her eyes told him again.

The shriek of a whistle to his left jerked him out of the dream, as he looked at his watch. Five thirty precisely. He blew for all his worth into his whistle as he began to climb the ladder.

He reached the top of the greasy, muddy, ladder and looked both ways to see infantryman spilling over the top of a trench like an overflowing river. The true power of the noise and din caught him as it did all the inexperienced boys who were with him. A noise so violent that it almost knocked one down. As he found his feet he found himself standing, in full view of the enemy, along with over a thousand of his fellow soldiers. As they looked in front they caught the momentary glimpse of the red flashes in the air which were the machine gun rounds approaching them. So fast and so many, almost covering every inch of air space. A score of Maxim machine guns each firing five hundred rounds per minute. The effects were devastating as the first wave of flying death crashed into the bodies of the

English Infantry. All at once they hit, taking whichever party of a body they hit with them as they flew through the ranks. The smacking sound as they hit clothed flesh was matched by the ping as they hit tin. Tin soldiers, they all fall down!! Chunks of flesh flew around the field, parts of skulls, hands, feet, bodies perforated, flying around. Everything a haze, waiting for nothing but death. The sound, Rat..tat..tat..tat..tat..tat……

'Down, Down!!' His voice was hardly audible, those who followed his instructions immediately did it involuntary. 'Down!'

They all hit the deck soon enough. The cries of agony were met with the cries of horror of those not yet hit. The obvious thought struck them all, 'what the fuck do we do now.' The rounds continued coming in like a horizontal rain storm, men trying not to get wet. The men picked whatever hunks of flesh lay in front of them for protection. The entire brigade was on the floor, no further than twenty yards from their own front line, still some one hundred yards from the objective.

Mercer was amazed to find himself unhurt as he tried to push his face as far into the muddy soil as he could. His uniform was splattered with pieces of his comrades who seconds before were standing by him. Before him would be a shell hole. He mustered the courage to put one bended arm in front of another as he crawled towards the haven of protection that was a ten foot mini ditch.

Upon arriving he breathed for the first time since leaving the trench. The only thought in his mind, the thought he always had when going over ... FUCKING HELL…Not again, I just can't do this again. He was joined by some half dozen soldiers, all wide eyed and somewhat disbelieving. Still above them was the hail of bullets, almost like a train running over them, the noise no less deafening. More joined, perhaps twenty now, all trying to bury themselves deeper. Although the instinct was to keep his head down, something urged him to look up and survey the situation. To both his annoyance and delight he saw that the Germans had got out of their trenches and stacked the Maxims on the parapets. As the hails above subsided he realised they had begun firing further North, assuming the entire line at his part had been disposed of. Across to his left he saw a line of men meet with a similar fate as his battalion had suffered, but this gave him a momentary opportunity. A line of machine gunners now were side on to him. After shouting at the top of his voice and kicking some men to regain their attention, he organised a line of five men and himself with a borrowed rifle to take aim against the line of machine gunners, now practically in the open. Their fire would attract further attention from these gunners but the plan was for each man to try to let off at least four rounds before retribution was upon them. 'You must aim, don't just shoot, you must aim'. They opened fire. Three machine gunners fell, rounds ricocheted off the guns and German bodies and to the amazement of the British, this small volley made the Germans run back into their trenches. Top British musketry at its best again. The dozy cowardly fuckers must have thought they had a machine gun rigged up. This gave them a good opportunity to get further towards the Germans in range for hand bombs which each Infantryman carried. Billy's weapons were a few bombs, his pistol which at this range was useless, a trenching tool, which he always took with him for close quarter combat, his borrowed rifle, whose dead owner did not seem to object to him taking and his fucking whistle! This was his chance. 'Right lads let's go now, if we stay here, we're all dead men.' He was on his feet and running for another crater which would bring them within thirty yards of the German lines. Surprisingly they were still not directly fired upon, their major concern was the shells which were still landing among them, turning men to dust or taking limbs with the shrapnel. He felt the presence of men beside and behind him, a larger number than he expected. But then these were British soldiers, the bravest men on earth, England's best. It seemed the entire remnants of his decimated battalion had followed him, roaring on to the objective he had set. Finally the Germans opened fire at devastating range, taking scores of men, but, again, leading his charmed life, Billy arrived in another shell hole, to be followed by a considerable number of surviving Infantrymen. 'Bomb the bastards' was the cry as over a dozen round balls were launched into the air. A second wave went over, their explosions barely audible in the din. These bombs seemed to be having some affect as the fire above seemed less intense. They maintained their meagre but steady flow of bombs with each man only guessing at what was happening in the formally constructed trench yards away from them. But certainly the flow of enemy fire seemed to have lessened. Now came the hard part. The final assault into the enemy trenches. This was the only way of defeating the enemy, get inside their trench and become a fanatical killing machine. High explosive artillery rounds then fell ahead of them, the British barrage opening up again on the Germans after hearing erroneous reports that the attacking force had been entirely wiped out. These rounds helped as the Germans retreated into dugouts inside their own trench networks. Rather good military tactics these, only they were by complete accident rather than design. Billy thought of his strategy. He had about thirty men with him. As soon as this barrage lifted he would lead his men in a mad charge of some twenty five odd yards into the enemy trenches. The distance of a cricket pitch. Like running between the wickets on a Sunday afternoon against the arm of a deep-fine-leg fielder whose throw from the boundary was one's opponent in the race to the crease. Not quite! Some of the rounds were falling short, near to his position, which was beginning to cause concern. After a wait of only minutes, the sound of the guns abruptly ceased. Billy took his pistol in his left hand, his entrenching tool in his right and led the fateful final charge. Gooooooo, which turned to an Aarghhh to a mad scream that all fighting men omit when charging at what would probably be impending doom. As soon as they rose, Billy saw the sandbags packed on the side of the trench with a six inch square hole in the middle. He saw hands fumbling behind it, a muzzle protrude through and then the dreadful machine gun spoke again. At such close range the rounds took large sections of flesh with them as they ripped through Billy's advancing comrades. Still he was not hit as the distance between he and the trench became less and less. Still men fell .Screams around him told him that a large proportion of his surviving force was hit. Rifle fire now, faces appearing over the parapet, shooting at his small force like shooting geese. Only yards to go. Billy shot a few rounds with his pistol, raised his trench tool over his head, hoping to jump over the sand bags and swing down on the occupants behind with one movement. Still he was not hit. He jumped, swung and landed over the trench with his tool pleasingly stuck in the back of the machine gunners neck. His colleague who feeds the gun tried to grab for his bayonet which was in his belt, only to find a pistol barrel pushed into his eye and a round take his brain away. Billy fell to the bottom with two dead men around him expecting to be immediately shot by at least one of the riflemen. No such fate as he discovered his fellow soldiers had reached this point and had begun their hand to hand fight with the German defenders. More British fell into the trench beside him wanting only German blood. By the time Billy was on his feet, the small section of trench, some twenty five feet of it before the next traverse, was his. His men were busily bayoneting the remaining German defenders who were putting up rather weak resistance.

Had other units penetrated the German lines or was Billy's force alone? This would have been useful information, but now the killing of Germans must begin in earnest. Traverses were in these trenches to prevent one shell from spitting its contents across the entire trench line, but they gave excellent assistance to an attacking force in this trench warfare. It was now the task to take the next section, then the next and hopefully meet up with fellow British soldiers, consolidate and hold the line. Billy had eight men with him, some of whom were continually bayoneting dead Germans. Without issuing further instructions, Billy rushed to the next section and his men followed. As he arrived he found half a dozen Germans almost expecting their arrival. His frenzy, almost drunken lust for blood charged him on. He could not stop for breath. With the sharp pick of his entrenching tool, he dived on the closest German as rifle fire exploded around him. Again, he should have been shot, but wasn't. 'On, On you noblest English!' His boys were behind him, both inspired and horrified by the actions of their captain. Without actually swinging his tool, Billy pushed the pick into the face of the closet German as both fell to the ground. The momentum of the fall was enough to push the pick through his facial skull, only stopping when it reached the inside of his skull on the other side of his head. Squirting blood greeted Billy as he pulled the tool out looking desperately for more prey. Rifle fire was around him along with screams as bayonet punctured bodies lay all over this section of the trench. The remaining Germans tried to run to the next section, but were cut down as they tried. Billy was busy slamming his tool into another helmeted skull, again and again he struck, looking for more and more blood. His face and uniform were now covered entirely with lumpy dark red and his hands were slimy with flesh material beneath his nails. He picked up a rifle bayonet which was abandoned on the ground and charged to the next section. Again they followed, becoming more uneasy with the reckless leadership of Mercer. To consolidate the present position would have been a better strategy, but Billy was unstoppable, like a fox in a chicken pen. He craved more death. At the corner of the next section he used his pistol to take two immediately out, as a young German fell to his knees and begged in clear English to be allowed to surrender. Billy walked past him and for a moment he believed he was spared. Billy then turned around, pulled his chin up from behind and with his knife cut deep into the young man's throat, so deep he felt the blade cut into his spine. The man's head was almost off as he slumped down, spraying the surrounding British with bright red blood. This was real war; this was hand to hand fighting. The remaining Germans in the section realised surrender was useless and tried to fight with their own tools, but the impetus was with the British. They had now taken over one hundred yards of trench with only a handful of men. This was commendation stuff of the highest order, they would all be decorated for this, if only they could make their commander stop now and wait for re-enforcements. But no, not a bit of it. Billy wanted more. A Corporal touched his shoulder in an attempt to begin dialogue. Billy turned, mad eyed and charged at the man pushing him to the ground. He took his knife ready again to cut his throat, only realising he was British after a small cut had been made. He immediately was on his feet charging to the next section, in hardened, blood curdling rage, when, from nowhere, he saw……her face. In the midst of this he saw, in his mind her face. I must see her again, he thought as he paused. At that time a small section of Germans came round the corner, determined to put up a better fight. The British stopped behind their leader. 'What now Sir?'

He didn't hear the rifle round, he only heard the crash inside his head, as loud as anything he had heard, as it went suddenly dark and the sounds around him completely ceased. He fell into a wet part of the trench beyond the duckboards, his eyes open, his face into a muddy puddle which quickly turned from brown to deep red. A huge gaping hole covered the back side of his head, his emotionless face staring into the wall of the trench as fighting men's boots, British and German trampled around his face. He was still, he was motionless. He was…

Chapter 27

Another day had passed but the torture of the previous night's sleep had somehow revolved during the morning into a deep inner calm. This sense was due to the total realisation of what must happen now. She had no choice whatsoever. She must leave her husband and spend every minute with Billy. The associated scandal carried as much significance as a minor consideration such as the choice of curtains for their new home. She had to be with him, she had to regularly lie with him, and she must give herself entirely to him, just him. She felt again like Juliet.

'And all my fortunes at thy foot I'll lay and follow thee my lord throughout the world.'

Unable to touch any breakfast, she wandered into the drawing room, grateful of its emptiness as it provided a perfect place to sit and think about him. As she sat a smile appeared on her face again which was interrupted by the sound of men's voices from outside the room. Her husband was with some staff officers speaking in concerned voices as they opened the door.

'Excuse us will you my dear, would you mind leaving us alone in here for a while?' her husband seemed strangely polite.

Wanting nothing more than to be away from this lot, she rose and walked past them. As she did so she caught a glimpse of one Colonel Price. He caught her gaze and gave her an extraordinary look. It was a look of slight smugness and superiority as if he was bursting with information which may be interesting to her. Noticing this made her curious. She waited in the hallway outside the drawing room with an immense feeling of foreboding. She just knew something was wrong. She approached the closed door, stretching her neck so her ear was closer. The aristocratic voices carried well.

'Colonel, thank you for coming from France so quickly, but thank you again for coming with such news.'

'May I offer you my congratulations Sir? Your plan, which I may mention was not widely welcomed', Price eyed a major among the group 'has proved a great success.'

'Against huge opposition, we broke through the line and the 3rd Battalion advanced more than half a mile. Casualties have been significant but you have achieved the impossible Sir'.

'We have consolidated the line eventually and now hold the drier ground. I'm sure General Haig will be delighted to hear this and I'm sure the King will wish to speak with you about it.'

Price was more interested in the decorations he may get for this action, as he bravely sat half a mile from the action reading reports from bloodied runners. 'I'd say it was one of the more successful brigade offensives of the past two years.'

A broad grin appeared on the General's face. At last he has been involved in a success in this war. He smugly edged towards the French windows and looked at his finely manicured lawn, along with the fine figure of a young gardener pushing a barrow across it.

'Casualties Colonel?' he continued admiring the youth.

'Well as I mentioned rather high. The first wave attacked at 5.30 and broke into the German trenches. This wave consisted of four companies. C company of my 3rd Battalion under Captain Mercer were the first to enter the trench.'

Her attention was captured like a dog will start at the sound of distant barking. He had made it back, somehow had made it back to take part in the offensive which he knew was doomed. Allowing herself to dream, she thought he may have never returned to the front and she would see him soon. But no, he had gone back.

The General's face hinted disapproval of the mere mention of his name.

'C company suffered seventy five killed and twenty two wounded out of the compliment of a hundred and eighteen.'
She froze.

'And Captain Mercer?'

'He was killed sir.'

Her legs seemed to give way as she reached for the wall for support. Michele was not there for support. Nobody to hold her as Melissa attempted to get away from the hall trying for some inexplicable reason to keep as quiet.

Chapter 28

The Rolls Royce was surely the Prince among cars in the early 20's. With its gleaming metal panels and purring engine the car approached the hospital and stopped by the grand front door. A resplendent chauffeur sprang from the car and opened the passenger door where an elegant lady with a young boy alighted into the frosty morning air. Melissa was as beautiful as ever. Her face showed the scars of emotional turmoil which added a distinction to her perfectly crafted features. A young porter stopped in his tracks to admire her as her little boy jumped up into her warm silver fox coat and she picked him up into her arms and kissed his three year old face. He wriggled and pointed at nothing in particular but his mother showed interest in the metal fence that his hand had picked out. His hair was blond and his eyes were blue and his mother adored him. His clothes were also of the finest quality but his mischievous face seemed somehow out of place in such refinement.

The chauffeur closed the door from which they came and climbed back into the front seat, driving away from the entrance. He would look forward to a time on his own, parked up outside the military hospital which housed the infirmed and badly wounded soldiers of the Great War. Wounded in ways that few understood. Most were beyond help and just received palliative care. Some were shell shock victims for whom no cure could be offered, but most were brain damaged, needing constant care and attention. This is the other side of war. This is the side devoid of glory. No heroic tales of dashing daring acts here. No Royal visits. No speeches or brass bands or jovial leaving parties. No, not here. Just bed pans, vomit, incontinence, screaming at night, irritable matrons and distant rarely seen doctors. What to do with the flotsam and jetsam from the great victory. What to do? Put them in a place like this one and wait for them to die. Let the visitors come once or twice. They usually do not come too often, although some patients have young women who sit by them with red eyes looking for glimpses of the men they once knew. A sad, dark and lonely place.

The smell of disinfectant greeted them both as they entered the main doors. Little Edward was walking now holding her hand. 'Pooo!' He shouted. 'Sssshhhhhh' she told him, 'quiet now darling.'

An officious matron rapidly approached the two of them, slowing somewhat when she noticed the quality of the attire on show. Melissa was always amused by the way people would change their behaviour towards her when they realised the station she held in life. Most people. Not one though. There was one who was never impressed by such things. Petulant little bugger he was.

'Can I help you Madam?' the matron asked, her eyes drawn to the beautiful quality of shoes that this elegant lady was wearing.

'Good morning Matron. Yes. Yes you can.'

The child was in her arms again as they entered the large room. It was probably a very nice drawing room at some time, but no longer. There were a dozen men, all in soft chairs facing the large French windows that offered views of the frosted valley below.

Some were making noises, one was talking to a friend that was not there, most were silent. The matron took them around a centrally placed table towards a corner area where a man was sitting with a tartan blanket over his legs. He was gazing out of the window, with the vacancy that seemed shared by most of the patients.

'Over there madam, and please, don't expect too much.'

'Thank you.' she said without looking at her. Her thoughts were elsewhere, her heart pounding like a drum. The matron reluctantly withdrew, intrigued by the nature of this visit. But it was none of her business, go away woman!

The low watery winter sun beamed through the windows, augmented by the reflections from the white frost covered ground. The light blinded her for a moment as she approached the figure and all was obscured. As she continued past the window the beams reduced and again her vision was resumed. Resumed to see him. Him, the man who was the first person on her mind when she woke and the last when she slept. The man who was back with her in her dreams and disappeared when she woke. But this was no dream; he was in her company again. Her quest was complete, she had found him.

It was only after a year when the memorial was opened to the regiment that she found his name was not included. It appeared at first that this was another of her husband's cruel and vicious punishments that she must endure and his name was deliberately omitted, in an attempt to pretend the man had not existed. His cruelty was intense after the breakdown she suffered on news of his death. This confirmed his suspicions and his anger grew in proportion to her despair. On one drunken evening he even took his pleasure from her as was 'his right.' This was again more of a punishment, as his enjoyment in this area was now confined to young willing soldiers looking for easy promotion.

It was only when Melissa went herself to the regimental headquarters in an attempt to include his name that she was told. He was indeed thought dead, his hideous wounds believed to be fatal. But, while lying with the dead, a young corporal saw some movement and patched his wound. This was the corporal who would receive the Military Medal for his part in the action which produced Mercer's injuries. The corporal had only followed orders and was almost killed by Mercer himself, but he held him, took care of him, taking him to the clearance station himself when all others slept. He admired Mercer, a true military leader. He almost attacked a medical orderly who independently declared Mercer beyond help and unworthy of a place in the casualty clearance station. Whatever there was left of Mercer's life, he had saved it.

Mercer was reported as killed, news welcomed by the staff, but news of his survival did eventually reach them but none chose to tell her. It had taken this time for her to find him, learn all about his actions, learn from the young corporal who was now a full Lieutenant who would tell stories of Mercer until the day he died.

Melissa had found him and was coming to see him. Melissa had someone to show him.

There he sat. His thick mousy hair was gone, replaced by thin strands of lifeless and unnecessarily long grey brown hair. The hair only covered part of his head as the back right side was removed. A large indented scab filled area covered what used to be the back of his head. How ugly it looked, almost unbearable to observe. O you poor man.

But it was him. Melissa was again looking at him. The moment that she believed would never come had arrived. The body of the man who owned her heart completely was there. But the whole man was not. She put down her boy and approached him. With small steps Melissa approached his right side walking in front to see his face again. His eyes remained fixed on the gardens outside, seemingly not noticing the presence of another. His deep blue almost violet eyes. The violet eyes of her son. His son. Unable to restrain herself, she held his head in her arms and held it tight, kissing his face tenderly.

'I am here my love, I've found you again. My dear, dear love, my life.' The dam in her eyes broke as tears came streaming down.

Still he did not respond. Eyes fixed on the windows, unable to react or even look at her. His mind, his personality was not present. Like a grand dance hall that once staged the best parties in England but was now a decrepit, cobweb filled, condemned shell. That is what Billy's body was now. But still she loved him.

How could the same face contain such a former life and yet be now devoid of expression. His face was worse than a painting, indeed a painting of him would have been a more accurate depiction of the man he was.

Saliva built up on his lips as he dribbled onto his lap. A sympathetic nurse was at hand to wipe it from him as the shock of his condition finally dawned on Melissa.

'He has not shown any emotion in three years Madam, never reacts to anything. His injuries are so very bad Madam, please don't expect him to respond.' The nurse paused as she saw Melissa's tears.

'Such a fine man, did you know him before the war? I always wonder what he would have been like. I hear he was a real hero' her insensitivity met with no response from Melissa as the nurse slowly withdrew, making eyes to the ceiling at the returning Matron.

Melissa again held his face. Held on to that lovely face which she had sometimes found difficult to recall. There were some regimental photos that she kept of him for her darkest moments, all that included his smile, but his face was not how she truly remembered him in those. Holding his face again she rocked from side to side with a pained smile on her beautiful face. She could detect his smell again, faint but still traceable. This was the same man, somewhere deep inside was her Billy, Her man. Her only man forever and ever and ever. Thoughts of what could have been returned to her again. Painful thoughts, such painful thoughts.

'I have someone to show you my love.' She beckoned Eddie over to her, who reluctantly obeyed walking towards the scary man in the soft chair. She picked him up and placed him on Billy's lap. The nurses looked on, beginning to realise what may be happening here.

Little Eddie's blue eyes looked into those of his Father's, those which had an identical hue. For a brief moment there was a flicker in Billy's eye, which vanished as quickly as it appeared.

'Mummy' Eddie said in a pleading shrill voice. She took him down and he stood behind her.

'He is your boy Billy, your boy. We made him together you and I. He's just like you, he is always naughty, always laughing and my whole life. I have some of you with me always now. He will be a great man like his dear Father. My husband actually thinks he's his son can you believe, and proudly parades him to everyone. But he's ours and he will have everything this life has to offer. He will never be a soldier he will be safe and will rise as high as you would have done my dear love. I will be by his side until the day I die and every time I look at him I will see you my darling love. I would not change a single thing, you brought me such happiness and the few moments we had will never leave me. You are my only love always my dear, always.'

She whispered the words in his ear as she held him in her arms. One more embrace, one more look, one more kiss. She kissed his motionless unresponsive lips and stood up. Still no response from the seated soldier. In one swift movement she turned, took her son's hand and walked away, leaving him still gazing. As he stared a single tear welled up in his right eye and followed a trail down his cheek onto his now dry mouth. Still he gazed.

The sound of a revving engine broke the silence as the car drove away, never to return.

She turned to her friend, once her maid, almost as in consideration saying, 'I know that I truly cherished every moment I spent with him. I am lucky in being able to say that. I have no need to feel I wasted a single moment with him, for even then, as I looked in his face, I realised how much I truly loved him and how my heart was burning . Although I miss him, at least I know I made the most of each minute with him. It was impossible not to. I can almost see him now before me. When I talk or think of him I feel the warmth of him again, him that brought love to me for the first time. I will never love another; my heart belongs to him and him alone. O God, how I loved him.'

The two women sat together reminiscing on the old times, the times when so much happened.

At that stage her words broke and she cried uncontrollably.

Chapter 29

The trip was arranged with all the best intentions in the world. To take the veterans to the place where they served seemed such a good idea. Many of them of course do not understand what day it is and such a trip is worthless but it was deemed suitable to take them along. Of the thirty veterans most could walk without assistance, although all had lost a good part of their mind psychologically or in Billy Mercers case, physically.

Mr Trancet, the director of the hospital had never seen the battlefields and it gave him a tremendous boost to experience them, along with men who actually fought here. Trancet had some of his own unique theories and ideas on rehabilitation. He would bore the staff regularly with his opinions on each patient. But he was not a doctor, he was a hospital director so very little attention was paid to his observations. However, his was a bright and happy face whose over enthusiasm could not be masked. He climbed out of the coach, took a deep breath of the Picardy air and surveyed the ground in front of him which was still scarred by the dreadful goings on almost fifteen years previously. At least it could never happen again. All the scare tactics the papers use about Mr Hitler could never convince him that mankind could sink so low again.

The group was unloaded from the coach, the last of whom was carried off and placed back into his wheeled chair. His young nurse did not care much for pushing him around a muddy field but the ground seemed hard enough. She was a pretty young thing who ideally preferred conventional nursing but was told the board at St Mary's would look favourably upon an application from an old soldier's mental infirmary. Hers was the job to take care of a poor man who had the back right side of his head almost missing and as such was practically a vegetable, waiting only for God. It was hard to imagine what he had looked like before his horrific injuries. It was clearly pointless bringing Mr Mercer back here, a man who has lost all his sensory perception, not knowing whether it is night or day, hardly even capable of swallowing. But she doesn't make the rules just merely does as she's told.

After a brief walk they stopped by a small copse while the guide explained which regiment was here or there and did this or that.

After his boring monologue the nurses gathered for a cigarette leaving the patients sitting on the grass, those in chairs facing the old front. Whilst a number of the men were oblivious to everything it seemed that a few did realise where they were and seemed curiously at peace. Mr Mercer sat looking at the copse, silently staring. The surroundings had certainly had an effect on him as his gaze suggested a deep understanding. For some twenty minutes he was left gazing until his eyes flickered to release a tiny tear which slowly flowed down his prematurely wrinkled face. Still he gazed, in a world all of his own. His hand flickered on the arm of his chair, his face expressing his recognition of these surroundings. Again his hand jumped as his arm slowly rose up as if to point ahead.

These actions were remarkable owing to the fact that he had hardly moved of his own accord in fifteen years. He now moved his head and turned to his nurse, who was no longer there but chatting some ten yards away, slowly drawing on her cigarette. He pointed to an area by the trees and spoke.

'I served here, I lived in a dugout just here for six weeks.' Despite the astonishment of his actions, nobody heard or turned to acknowledge him.

'Just here,' as he turned back, still pointing at what was now merely a shallow ditch.

'Eddie was killed here, my friend Eddie.' These words were matched with activity in his legs as slowly but surely he rose to his feet.

Still nobody noticed, nobody came over to steady him, they continued smoking almost as if to deliberately ignore him. Still pointing, he took a step towards the copse, continually turning in anticipation of a response from his carers but still nothing.

Miraculously he walked towards the copse, getting stronger with every step. Slowly his back seemed to straighten, his shoulders seemed to unfold and a youthful look came about his face. His terrible scars even seemed less visible as he continued on his march towards the trees, now only fifty yards away. He turned to his party who were still oblivious to him, taking no notice at all.

Strong and straight he was as he continued his approach. To his surprise he heard voices from within the copse, jovial English voices, the type of voice so familiar to him from his younger days. His pace quickened as he got nearer and then caught a glimpse of a figure from behind the bushes. Not one but suddenly two, then three. As he gazed he could see a group of young men standing around, smoking, laughing, chatting still obscured by the branches of the young elder trees. The sun broke free from the confines of a summer cloud and lit up the copse like a flare. It was suddenly warm as again he checked on his party, now some sixty yards away. Compelled he was, to continue into the wood, to join these men. From just outside he noticed the figure of a blond man in the full uniform of an English infantry Lieutenant, but an officer from the Great War. As the figure turned it became familiar, the hair, the stature almost like, not like but it actually seemed to be…Eddie. He brushed the branches away as the entire group of ten men turned to greet him. All in uniform, mostly privates, a few stripes here and there. All looking resplendent, handsome, young, happy, at peace. However these were not just young men. These were his friends. All in a line they were, faces beaming, young small Bobby, no longer scared but beaming, tall lanky Pete, Georgie, Jimmy, Charlie, the hilarious figure of the Kings Road Pipe smoking, of course, his pipe. Paulo was there, Johnny Mason, Reggie and, … and Eddie.

Eddie, how good it was to see him.

'We've been waiting for you', his stunning handsome face

smiling like Jesus to a child. Was it all a dream, could it be a dream, or better?

'My boys, my lads, it's been so hard without you, it's been so dark and so cold. It's been so long, so agonisingly long, all on my own. It's been so long.'

The power of the sun intensified all around both in heat and light as if to tell him it won't be dark any more. It will not be cold anymore. He glanced at his wrist and noticed he was again in full uniform. Three pips on each shoulder, Captain Mercer. His hair had grown, his face young again. The face she fell in love with. No longer a twisted damaged visage like an old tattered box.

'Come on young man, we'd like to take you somewhere we think you'll like,' and with a warm smile KRP put the pipe back in his mouth.

Off they walked, eastward, a band of brothers, arms around one another, so much to talk about, and so much to say.

The sun crept back behind a cloud as the group of nurses gathered around the old man in a wheeled chair, panicking as they drew on each other for guidance. Mr Trancet darting about, totally useless to anyone, his day ruined. 'There's no pulse' she said, 'no pulse.'

She was right, there was no pulse. But on the face of Mr Mercer was an intense, elated smile.

The End

Epilogue

The year was 1968. Fifty years to the day that the armistice was signed that ceased hostilities in the Great War. Dignitaries from every nation involved in the awful conflict were present for the large commemoration ceremony with Veterans and Royalty marking the date.

The British Prime Minister had taken his Mother, who, despite her seventy two years was still very active and attractive. Before the ceremonies began, he had made a diversion to a cemetery in France. He walked through the finely cut grass as the morning dew deposited tiny droplets which separated on the polish of his hand made Church shoes. He was tall and smart, with a hard face and piercing eyes. He was a Prime Minister who had garnered many of the electorate's female votes. He was walking with his Mother who was leading the way. Behind them were the countless security personnel, scanning the surrounding areas and communicating with those by the fleet of Jaguar Cars which awaited the return of them all.

They walked among the snow white gravestones each of which detailed the life of a fallen soldier from 1914-18. They were in perfect lines, straight and erect, almost on parade, resplendently clean and proud. They walked to the far end and the lady stopped by two graves that were at the end of a line. The Prime Minister stopped and looked at the stone that had her attention. It read 'Lt Edward Tompkin' and had the Fusilier badge above the words, deeply chiselled into the white stone. Her head turned to the adjacent stone that formed the end of the line. It also had the Fusilier badge but the name below read

'Capt William Mercer MC MM'

Finally he was lying by his friend. She had seen to that. She took her son's hand and he looked down at his Mother.

He was proud of her and proud of the life she had led and the sacrifices she had made on his behalf. He smiled a loving smile at his Mother and looked back at the stone.

His Mother touched the stone of Mercer, kissed her fingers and touched it again.

The Mother and Son stood for several minutes, neither talking. Finally he turned and motioned to his assistant. He held his Mother as if to support her as they walked back to the fleet of awaiting vehicles.

Paradoxically, Rt Hon Edward Wilton PM was very happy. Very happy and proud.

Lightning Source UK Ltd.
Milton Keynes UK
UKHW02f1007061217
313973UK00014B/815/P